D1411775

Tom's Revenge and Other Stories for Children
Character Classics volume six

Printed in U.S.A.
Cover art: James Converse

Tom's Revenge
and
More Stories for Children

The stories in this book were complied from two different series, Sunshine Stories and Sabbath Readings. These stories were originally gathered from church papers in the 1870's, Methodists, Lutheran, Presbyterian, etc. We have found the stories to be truly "a breath of fresh air" in literature for children and youth. May they receive a warm welcome in your home is our prayer.

The Publishers.

A. B. Publishing
3039 S. Bagley
Ithaca, Mi 48847

Contents

Tom's Revenge 7
A Story for Boys 11
Hard to Be Good 15
Sails of a Vessel 17
Follow Copy 19
Indecision 20
What Ruined Him 25
The Sister's Lesson 30
Hasty Words 38
Angry Words 45
Flossy and His Mistress 51
The Orphans 63
"Girls, Help Father" 67
May and Might 71
Outward Appearance 75
The Cross Family 85
Taking a Situation 98
Where the Gold Is 105
"I Will Do It" 109
The Little Weaver 117
The Garden of Peace 122
She Is Unkind to Her Mother 125

Tom’s Revenge

“I hate Ned Lane,” said Tom Bixby, doubling his fists and stamping his feet. “He’s a mean, spiteful, wicked boy. I wish he were dead, I do!”

Then Tom broke down and fairly burst into tears. His mother, who had heard his angry words, came out to the garden to see what had caused them. She too, was indignant at what she saw. There was Tom’s pet dog, Fawn, stretched out cold and stiff on the grass. Around his neck a string was tied, from which dangled a card. On it these words were written in a scraggy, blotted hand: “He’ll never chase my chickens no more.—Ned Lane.”

“Oh Mother!” cried Tom, “look at poor, poor Fawn; see what that cruel Ned has done. Oh, how I hate him. I’ll be revenged.”

Fawn had been a favorite with the Bixby family, and in spite of the fact that he would pursue chickens and tear the dresses of passing ladies or catch and hide away stockings and handkerchiefs when they were laid upon the grass to bleach, Mrs. Bixby had borne with him. She had hoped that his youthful faults would be cured in time. She knew that Ned Lane had been very angry because of the loss of two rare fowls, which Fawn had shaken and torn to pieces, and she felt that Fawn had been a great annoyance to the neighbors—a great transgressor.

But what to do with Ned was the question, for Tom's heart was almost broken.

"Tom," she said, "you say you hate Ned. Do you wish, what I heard you say just now, to be really avenged?"

"Yes, Mother, I want to see him suffer; I wish all his chickens were gone."

"Ned has done a cruel deed, and I do not wonder that you are deeply grieved; but, my son, he that hateth his brother is a murderer."

"He's not my brother."

"In one sense he is; yet I am sure you do not mean that you would really like to see him dead and cold like your dog. If you think of the meaning of your words, I am sure you wish him no such ill. I think there is a way by which you can make him very sorry for this and yet keep your own self-respect."

The gentle tones won their way to Tom's heart. He sat down by his mother, and she passed her soft hand over his hot brow and soothed him tenderly. Then she gave him her plan for being "quits," as he called it, with Ned, and for getting the victory.

The next day, when Ned Lane met Tom Bixby on his way to school, he was rather mortified to hear nothing about Fawn. He was prepared to defend himself if attacked. But Tom passed in silence. He tried to say "Hallo, Ned!" but failed in the attempt. All the morning, however, when the boys were in the classes together, Tom looked and acted as usual, and at recess he engaged heartily in games with the other boys.

When Ned, feeling more and more uncomfortable, went home to dinner, a surprise awaited him. A superb pair of Brahma-pootra fowls had arrived, with a string and card attached: "For those my poor Fawn chased. —Tom Bixby."

I cannot say truly that the two from this time, became fast friends; but this I know Ned Lane was thoroughly ashamed of his mean and unworthy action, and never after was guilty of the like cruelty, while Tom felt, even at Fawn's grave, that forgiveness is sweeter than revenge.

"To err is human, to forgive, divine."
"Teach me to feel another's woe,
To hide the fault I see;
That mercy I to others show,
That mercy show to me."

A Story for Boys

"I'll be even with him yet," muttered Fred Eaton, as he entered the hall, flushed with anger, and threw his books and cap upon the table. The study door stood open, and as Fred was rather demonstrative in his feelings, the noise he made penetrated into the study and reached Mr. Eaton's ears.

It was no unusual thing for Fred to be noisy; boys generally are; but there was a certain spitefulness in his manner that made his father think something extraordinary had happened. He called him into the study.

"Why, my son, what is the difficulty? You appear very much excited."

"It's enough to make anyone provoked," blurted out Fred, getting, if possible, still redder in the face.

"It must be something very serious," said Mr. Eaton, "to have such an effect upon you. Let me hear the story."

"Well, Father, you know the creek that runs through Mr. Cheeseman's lot. We boys had divided ourselves into two parties and were having a mimic fight on the water. We have been all the week building the dams and making the boats, and tomorrow the fight was to come off."

"Well, what is to hinder? I envy you the sport you will have and almost wish I were a boy again."

"Jim Tracy is commander of the British fleet, and I was appointed to command the Americans. Ben Jones was to load and fire my cannon—that beauty you gave me last Fourth of July. Every boy had some part to perform, and Ben insisted on being the 'gunner.' We rigged our boats this morning and had a sort of rehearsal during recess. The bell sounded when we were in the midst of our fun, but Ben insisted on having another charge at the enemy. I knew it wouldn't do, and I spoke rather sharply to him, I confess. I told him it was my cannon, and he had no right to touch it without my consent, and he'd better put it down. He was very angry and, out of spite, put in a double charge and burst my little cannon all to pieces. I was so angry, Father, I felt as though I could have torn him in pieces on the spot. But I'll be even with him yet," added Fred, after pausing long enough to take a breath.

"Ben was certainly a bad boy; but I am afraid Fred Eaton's temper is none of the best, and under the same circumstances he might have been tempted to do even worse than Ben did."

"Oh Father! I wouldn't have done such a thing for the world," said Fred, with open-eyed astonishment, at the bare mention of such a possibility.

"Perhaps not, but your feelings toward him were evidently worse than his towards yourself. For Ben only destroyed a cannon, that can be easily replaced, while you felt like tearing him in pieces."

"I didn't mean that exactly, Father; you know I wouldn't do it."

"It was Satan in your heart, and you gave him the use of your tongue. It is this wanting to 'get even' that has been the ruin of many. I am glad you thought twice and did not give vent to your wicked feelings before Ben Jones, for now you have advantage over him, and can teach him a lesson that may last him through life. At the same time you can be more than even with him."

Fred's eyes sparkled.

"I will give you money for another cannon this afternoon, a little larger than the other. When you go to school in the morning, be sure you see Ben alone and hand him the cannon. Tell him you have forgiven him, and you hope this cannon will prove stronger and last longer than the other."

"But he destroyed it on purpose," said Fred.

"And you can forgive him, I trust," said his father. "Do as I tell you, and let me know the result. I know you will feel better and happier after it. It is sweet to be able to forgive an injury, and make an enemy your friend."

You should have seen Fred when he came in from school the following day. His face was in perfect contrast to that of the day before, and he fairly bounded into the study.

"I did it, Father, I did it," he exclaimed; "we had a most royal time, and the Americans beat the British fleet, and I believe it was all owing to that cannon. How it did talk! At first Ben wouldn't take the cannon, but I insisted on it, for I really had forgiven him. He said he was sorry for what he did and looked so ashamed all the time that—that—"

"Well, how did Fred feel?"

"Why, Father, I felt like a conqueror."

"It is something to have gained two victories in one day," said Mr. Eaton, smiling.

Hard to Be Good

"Harry," said I to one of my most *wary* scholars, "you have been a very good boy. I hope you will do as well all the term."

"I'll try, Teacher," said Harry, with an audible sigh; "I'll try, but it's *awful hard work to be good.*"

"Ah, Harry," I thought, as he turned away, "you are not the first one who has found this out. To be good is uphill work for all, and the hill is so high and so steep that none can climb alone. If you try ever so hard, you will fail."

"Who will help me?" says one. "Who *can* help me better than myself? Why not depend upon myself in this as in other things?"

Because *you cannot* do this alone. Because there is one who will help you to be good, who *longs* to help you if you will but ask Him. Jesus, your Saviour, is His name. He says, without Me ye can do nothing (nothing good). It is *hard work* without Him, but go to Him, and you will find His yoke easy and His burden light. It will not then be so "hard work to be good."

Plant blessings, and blessings will bloom;
Plant hate, and hate will grow;
You can sow today—tomorrow shall bring

The blossom that proves what sort of thing
Is the seed, the seed that you sow.

Sails of a Vessel

One fine Sunday afternoon, Clara and her father were seated on the balcony of a hotel overlooking the sea, where they had come to spend a few weeks, and they enjoyed watching the great ocean, the waves of which broke at their feet.

Vessels of all shapes and sizes were sailing before them—some going north, some south—some lighted up by the sun, others under the shadows of the clouds, but all in movement.

"Father," said Clara, "I never could understand how the wind should drive the vessels in more than one direction at the same time. Look, there are two with their sails filled, and yet one is coming nearer to us, while the other is going away from us."

"Everything depends upon the way in which the sails are set," said her father, and he explained the various ways of setting the sails.

"It is just the same with men and their lives," continued he, "the same cause operates differently upon different individuals. To become rich makes one man generous and another mean. Sorrow hardens some and softens others. I have been thinking of poor Fred Merrill, who appeared to learn so much that is bad in the same school in which our Edmund was only taught good."

"I understand now," said Clara. "I remember going to church with one of my friends, and I was much interested in the sermon. I came out of church full of what I had heard and resolved to practice it. I was astonished when my companion said, 'What a stupid sermon! I thought it would never end!'"

"Yes, my dear," said her father, "the gospel itself saves some and condemns others. It is a solemn thought that every good we refuse is no good to us. Every warning that we attend to is a benefit, but if it is neglected we only grow hardened in evil. Every gift of God is good if we use it without abusing it. We ought to try to get some good out of every experience we have, and then we shall grow and be strong."

Follow Copy

A short time since, a lad in the printing office received from his master a list of Scripture questions and answers to be set up and printed. In the progress of the work, the lad turned aside and asked the foreman if he must "follow copy"; that is, set it up just as it was written.

"Certainly," said the foreman. "Why not?"

"Because this copy is not like the Bible, and it professes to be the language of that book."

"How do you know it is not like the Bible?"

"Why, I learned some of these texts at a Sabbath school, ten years ago, and I know that two of them are not like the Bible."

"Well, then, do not follow copy, but set them up as they are in the Bible."

The lad got the Bible, and made it "the copy," his guide and pattern.

"Follow copy," children, wherever you find it according to the Bible, but do not stir a step when you find it differs. Through all your life make the Bible your own copy. Look to your words, your actions, your doctrines, and your practices—see that all are according to the Bible, and you will be right.

Indecision

Any boy who understands machinery knows what it is when an engine is on a "dead center." Let us explain to those who do not understand. When the walking beam of a steam engine has lifted the crank to its highest point, or depressed it to its lowest, that point is called the "dead center." If the crank swings over as it usually does, then the rod goes down from the highest point and up from the lowest. But, sometimes when an engine is going slowly, the crank does not swing past the center, and then, as the piston presses straight down, or draws straight up, it does not tend to turn the crank as it does when in any other position, so the engine stops, and the crank has to be swung over the center by hand.

Now, this "dead center" is in an engine just what indecision is in a boy or man. The crank moves slowly and without force enough to carry it over that point. It is undecided which way to go, and it stops; and, till it can be started by extraneous force, the boat is at the mercy of the winds and waves. If a boy's mind moves slowly and in an undecided manner, his moral force—his engine—gets on a "dead center," and away he floats downstream.

Standing on the dock in one of our seaport towns, a large steamer getting under weigh could be seen. The current was running swiftly by the wharf and the river full of large shipping. The steamer cast off and swung out into the stream; the engine made three of four revolutions and then stopped. The pilot sounded the bell in the engine room to go ahead, but it was not answered. The boat drifted swiftly, and in a moment crash it went against a ship and carried away her rigging around her bowsprit; then smash it went into another steamboat and made a wreck of her wheelhouse and very badly damaging herself.

The pilot was frantic with rage at what he deemed the stupidity of the engineer; the officers of the craft were loudly cursing the stupidity of the pilot, and there was a great running to and fro of all hands, when the pilot was told by the engineer that his engine was on a "dead center," and till the crank was pushed in some way he was powerless. By this time the boat had drifted a long way and was almost a wreck. Indeed, so badly damaged was she that she could not go on her voyage, and in her drifting she had crippled several other crafts. The only remedy was to down the anchor, which the pilot did as soon as he saw that the engine was useless. But it was too late. The damage was done, and the boat was afterward hauled off for repairs.

A boy needs decision of character more than any other trait, and we can sympathize with a boy who is doing his best to cultivate this virtue. It is his sheet anchor, which, by the help and grace of God, can hold him right when all else fails him. A boy should learn how to say "No," and not only how to say it, but how to live up to it. "When sinners entice thee, consent thou not"; that means, say "No" with an emphasis, and, after saying "No," leave the place at once. It is your only safety. If you say, "Get thee behind me, Satan"; he won't "get." He never goes away politely and humbly when ordered—not he. He will face you, and the only way to get him behind you is to turn around and walk away, and then, of course, he is behind you. This requires decision.

If Tom and Harry tempt you to run away from school or go where you ought not to go, and you reply in an undecided way—"I guess not; perhaps it is not best; I rather think I'd better not" —you are Tom and Harry's boy. They have you for sure. If a boy is undecided, he is lost. But if, when they make such a proposition to you, you say "No," and turn away; why then you are safe, and neither Tom, Harry nor Satan has the least hold upon you. A boy who is undecided in his moral character, in his sports, —and—when he grows up in his business—floats, drifts along to sure destruction; for every craft that drifts is doomed.

If circumstances arise in which you question what course to pursue, remember that in such a case, there is a safe appeal which must result in accordance with the highest good. Namely, ask yourself what would the Saviour do under such circumstances; just what you suppose He would approve or advise, *that* you will be safe in doing. Do this, and there will be no "dead center," no indecision, no yielding to temptations.

How important that all, especially the young, make the application; don't wreck yourself and others by indecision; don't drift and float down the swift stream of life with all your energies on a "dead center." This is forcibly brought to mind when we see a man, who might do a great deal of good in every way, loafing though life, a curse to himself and to all about him.

Remember, the will to do rightly,
If used, will the evil confound;
Live daily by conscience, that nightly
Your sleep may be peaceful and sound.
In contests of right never waver,
Let honesty shape every plan,
And life will of Paradise savor,
If you do as near right as you can.

What Ruined Him

A young man, who was in prison awaiting his trial for a serious crime, was asked what ruined him.

"Sir," he replied with tears in his eyes, "it was my street education that ruined me! I had a good home education, but I would slip out of the house and go off with the boys in the street. In the street, I learned to lounge. In the street, I learned to swear. In the street, I learned to smoke. In the street, I learned to gamble. In the street, I learned to steal."

So you see, my dear children, the street ruined that youth. It seemed pleasant to him, as it does to some of you, to spend his hours abroad with idle, boisterous lads. No doubt he thought his father and mother were too strict, too particular, and notional, when they wished him not to frequent the street; and, thinking so, he chose to have his own way even at the price of disobeying his parents. He did have his own way. To what did it lead him? To destruction! I think he paid too high a price altogether for having his own way. Do you agree with me in this opinion? If so, beware how you imitate him, beware how you cherish a love for the street and street companions. Find your enjoyment at home, especially in the evening.

You may depend upon it, boys and girls, that to pass safely along the ways of life, you must be careful of your steps. It will not do for you to tread a path merely because flowers grow in it and you feel a desire to pluck them. The most flowery paths often lead to the most dangerous places. You must seek, therefore, for the right rather than for the pleasant way. Indeed, the right path is always the most pleasant in the end.

To find the right way, and thus to avoid the dangers of the wrong one, you need a guide for your feet. I have read somewhere, that on a part of the seashore in England, there are steep cliffs rising abruptly from the beach. To keep smugglers from landing foreign goods on which duties have not been paid, a guard is stationed to watch both night and day. The men composing this guard have to ascend and descend the cliffs in the night. Their path is very narrow, and it runs close to the edge of the cliff. A single misstep would cause a man to fall over on to the beach and to be dashed to pieces.

How do you suppose the men of that guard find their way up and down those cliffs at night in safety? If you were to examine their path, you would see a row of very white stones set in it all the way up from the beach. These stones can be seen in the darkest night. The men look for them and thus traverse the giddy path with safety.

Now, my dear children, God meant his Holy Book to be to you, on your life journey, what those white stones are to the men who guard that cliff in England. It tells you where to go and where not to go, what to do and what to avoid. If you wish, then, for safety, you must both study and obey the Bible. If you will not, why, like the young man in the prison, you must find pain, shame, and death in your pathway.

The Heart and Tongue

One Mr. Tongue, of much renown,
Who lived at large in Tattletown,
Was mischief full, and wicked too,
As all could tell, if Tongue they knew.

The statute brought the charge was plain,
That tongue was full of deadly bane.
Tongue then was seized, to court was brought,
Pleading himself the impending suit:

"'Tis neighbor Heart," plead Mr. Tongue,
Who leads me into so much wrong.
I should be good, as neighbors are—
As Mr. Nose, or eye, or ear—

"If neighbor Heart, who lives below,
Were changed by grace, or made anew,
'Tis very hard to bear the wrong
Of neighbor Heart," said Mr. Tongue.

The plea was sound of Mr. Tongue.
Jurors and Judge said, all as one
"While neighbor Heart is all so wrong,
No good, they said, could come from Tongue."

The Court decide, as the best good,
To renovate the neighborhood,
That Mr. Heart *must be renewed*,
Or never Tongue can be subdued.

The Sister's Lesson

"Oh dear! This noise is enough to drive on crazy. I can't understand a single word of what I am reading. Willie, you sit down here, and Lizzie, you take a seat right by the fire-place and don't speak another word for fifteen minutes."

So spoke Mary Wheeler, a young lady of sixteen, to her little brother and sister. After settling them each in a chair far enough from each other, she took her book and soon forgot all else in the interesting story.

Mother was out, and Mary had been left in charge to see that the little ones got into no mischief, and certainly there didn't seem to be much danger just now.

The room was perfectly quiet which a moment before had been ringing with merry shouts of laughter, and the little faces which had seemed so brimful of merriment had subsided into a half-fearful, half-pitiful expression. They looked longingly at each other and cast pleading glances towards their "big sister," but Mary's attention was entirely on the story. Just then she happened to be at the most exciting part.

Grandma was upstairs knitting by the parlor fire and listening to the merry laughter of the children.

She noticed the sudden cessation of sounds, and laying aside her work, went down to find the cause.

On opening the door, she was amused at first to see them sitting up so quietly in their chairs, but her countenance changed as she noticed the expression on the little faces.

"Mary," said she, in her gentle way, "will you come upstairs a little while with me?" Mary looked up, then longingly at her book, finally closed it, and went slowly to the door, where she turned back and said, "Children, you may get down now, but don't be naughty." When both were seated in the cozy parlor, grandma took her knitting, wiped her spectacles, put them carefully on her nose, looked up once or twice at Mary, who sat on the other side of the fire-place, and then said, suddenly, "Mary, do you remember when you were a child?"

"Why yes, Grandma, of course," said Mary, blushing; for she remembered that it was rather an unsettled point, in the minds of the elder members of the family, whether she were not one still. "Yes! It isn't so very long ago."

"I think," said her grandma, "that we are apt sometimes to forget that we were ever children. I had a lesson once, which, though it makes me sad when I remember it, still I think it has been a means of making me more tender and thoughtful of the little ones. If you have time to listen, I should like to tell it to you."

Mary began to wonder whether there wasn't what she termed "a lecture" coming pretty soon; but she answered respectfully, "Certainly, Grandma, I have plenty of time and should like to hear it."

"Well, my dear, it's forty-five years ago now, yet still I remember as though it were yesterday. I was your age, just past my sixteenth birthday, and the only sister of my two brothers—Harry, two years younger than I, and Charlie, a baby of three summers. I am sure I loved them both, especially the younger. I was proud of his beauty and pleased when strangers praised his sweet winning ways. One Friday afternoon, mother, father, and Harry went out, and Charlie and I were left at home. He took his blocks and began to build houses, and I seated myself in the easy chair by the fire, determined to finish all my lessons that day, so that the next, which was a holiday, I might have to enjoy as I pleased. I had studied perhaps half an hour and was deep in a problem of Euclid, when I felt a gentle pull at my dress, and Charlie's sweet voice said, 'Sister, sister, won't you play with me a little while?'

"'No, Charlie,' said I, 'run away now and don't trouble sister; she's busy'—and I went on with my lesson. He lingered a moment by my side, looked anxiously up in my face, then walked slowly away.

"It was not long before he was again by my chair. 'I'm tired. Won't you hold me on your lap just a little while, Sister Lizzie?'

"'No, Charlie, not now,' I said. 'Go look at your picture-book a while and don't trouble sister.' I thought I heard a sob as he turned away which almost persuaded me to let my lessons go until the next day; but no, thought I, by-and-by will do just as well. So I went on studying.

"The little fellow didn't disturb me anymore. Once or twice I heard a half sob, but they soon stopped, and the room was still. The sun, which had shone brightly into the room when I commenced my lessons, began to sink behind the distant hills. The light grew less and less, until I could scarcely see; but as the clock struck five, I closed my books, happy in the thought that tomorrow I could have to do with as I liked. I gathered up my slate and pencils, to put all in order, and turned to go toward the closet. The bright fire lightened the room, though it was quite dark without. As I turned, I saw my little brother laying fast asleep on the floor, with his curly head resting on his folded arm. How beautiful he looked with the firelight shining on him. How red his cheeks were. But as I stooped to lift him, I noticed that his breath came short and quick, and his face was very hot. I seated myself in the rocking chair, and placed his head gently on my shoulder. Suddenly he started up and looked wondering at me a moment—then said, 'Why, sister, you are holding me, aren't you? I dreamed I went to sleep on the snow, and it was so cold, but I'm warm now—real warm.' He nestled his pretty head again on my shoulder and fell asleep.

"A half hour later mother came home. 'Well, Lizzie, where's Charlie?'

"'Here he is, mother,' I said.

"She bent and kissed him. 'Why, how hot his lips are. He has not been out of the room, has he, Lizzie, in the cold?'

"'No, Mother,' I said, 'he has been here all the time.' She took him from me, undressed him and put him in his crib. At bedtime I went to bid him good night. Oh how hot his cheeks were as I kissed him.

"The next morning my mother came to my door to call me. 'Lizzie,' said she, 'Charlie is quite sick. You must get up and see to breakfast, while I stay with him. Jane has gone for the doctor.'

"How quickly I dressed and hurried into the room where my brother lay. He was delirious, and as soon as he saw me enter he called out, 'O sister Lizzie, *please* hold me; I'm so tired.'

"Oh how I wept. 'Yes, darling!' I said, I will hold you and sing to you.'

"The doctor came and said he was very ill and must be kept very quiet, so all but father and mother were forbidden the room. Oh how slowly that holiday passed by, and the Sunday and Monday following. The house seemed desolate when Charlie's sweet voice was not heard. Tuesday afternoon I came from school.

Father met me at the door: 'Lizzie,' he said, 'you know, of course, that Charlie has been very ill. The doctor says that you and Harry may go in a little while this afternoon and see him.'

"I uttered a cry of joy, and sprang toward the stairs. My father caught me back and strove to speak, but the words seemed to choke him. The tears were streaming from his eyes as he let me go and motioned me away. I did not run now, for I felt I was going to see my darling for the last time. As I entered the room and approached the bed where he lay, he turned his beautiful eyes toward me and smiled so sweetly as he said, 'O Lizzie, I'm so glad you held me. I dreamed that I was asleep on the cold snow.'

"The tears fell fast as I bent over him. 'Charlie,' I said, 'you won't leave sister, will you? You will let her hold you again and sing to you, won't you darling?'

"He looked bewildered a moment, then smiling said, 'No, I'm only going to sleep! I'm so tired you know.' I kissed the baby lips and felt his arms twine round my neck. Ah! What would I have given if I could only have gone back to that Friday afternoon and held the little form while I rocked him to peaceful slumber. But no. He unclasped his arms from my neck, glanced quickly at each who stood near him, then, fixing his eyes as though looking at something in the distance, his lips parted in a smile. Sobs filled the room as my mother closed the lids over his blue eyes, straightened out the limbs, and crossed the dimpled hands on his baby breast. 'He will never be tired anymore,' she said. Oh how the words sank into my heart. No! He will never need my care again. I could please myself without any interruption now. Little Charlie would never ask me to play with him again, and He who loved little children—who 'pleased not himself'—had taken away my baby brother as a lamb in His bosom.

"So, Mary, it is because I would save you from unhappy memories that I tell you this. Your little brother and sister may not die but live to be men and women; but be sure, for any kindness or sympathy you give them now, you will be amply repaid in the future by the love they will give you."

Grandma laid aside her knitting and wiped her eyes, and Mary put her arms softly around her neck as she said, "Thank you, Grandma, I will try and be more unselfish."

Lord, raise my youthful mind to see
How good it is to trust in Thee;
From all the enemies of truth,
Do thou, Great God, preserve my youth;
Free my young mind from worldly snares,
From youthful sins and youthful cares;
And in this heart, though hard as stone,
Let seeds of early grace be sown,
That finding pardon through my Saviour's
blood,
I may devote my youthful powers to God.

Hasty Words

"Mother, please look here and see my pretty blockhouse. When I'm a man we'll have one just like it."

I glanced at four-year-old Harry, who had constructed a most wonderful edifice in the middle of my sitting room.

"I am afraid it would not keep out much of the snow," said I.

"But it would be so nice in the summer," said Harry, laughing merrily and springing to my side. He threw his little arms around my neck, saying, "Oh, Mamma! I love you so!"

"Harry," said I, kissing him, "will you run and tell Bridget to have warm biscuits for tea?" He started quickly, and as he started his foot caught in a light stand upon which I had placed a rare Parisian vase, with a rose bud just unfolding its crimson petals in it. The stand fell over, and the vase (a gift from my dead mother) was shattered.

"You naughty boy," I cried angrily, "you deserve to be whipped. Pick up those pieces instantly, and put them in the coal hod." He stooped, and carefully picked up the fragments, cutting his fingers as he did so against the sharp edges. He carried them away and was gone some time. When he returned, it was with something clasped tightly in his hand.

Coming to me he placed a five cent piece in my lap, saying timidly, "Will that buy you a new vase, Mamma?"

What evil demon possessed me to take the coin, his sacredly cherished treasure (a kind neighbor had given him for some little office), and throw it from me, I know not.

Harry picked it up with tears running down his face, and sat down upon his stool with his hands folded so meekly. Presently he said, "May I go and play with Eddie Potter?"

"I don't care where you go," said I, crossly, "so you keep out of my sight."

Harry went to the closet where his coat and hat hung, put them on, and came and stood by my side.

"Mamma, will you please forgive me? I'm so sorry"; and he put his lips up for a kiss. I pushed the little fellow away. He stood by the door a moment, looking pitifully at me. It is twenty-five years ago today since he stood there, but I can see him with his blue coat and red and gray worsted skating cap and the little red mittens, as if it were but yesterday. But I looked coldly at him; the door opened and shut and the little feet went slowly down the stairs. I heard him go out and unfasten the gate. Looking out of the window, I saw the little fellow lift his face with a smile as he saw me, which gave place to a pitiful quiver of the lips as he saw I took no notice of him. I watched the darling down the street with a strange undefined feeling, till the little coat and red mittens were no longer visible. Twice a sudden impulse moved me to call him back, but I crushed it down. Oh, would to God I had! Well, I sewed all through the afternoon. At four o'clock I put away my work and sat by the window. Conscience began to reproach me for my conduct. "I don't care," said I, "my beautiful vase is a ruin."

"What is the value of all vases in the world compared to your child? Have you not spoken crossly to that dear little Harry, who is always so cheerful and obedient? And this is not the first time either, and you calling yourself a Christian mother, too? Suppose Harry should be taken suddenly from you. Wouldn't your cruel words haunt you forever?

I could bear this no longer. I rose, and picked up my stray litter about the room to give it a more tidy appearance.

Then I went to the window, peering anxiously through the gloom, but seeing nothing of my boy. My heart became terribly heavy; this suspense was unbearable. Hastily throwing a shawl over my head, I ran into Mrs. Potters'. "Have you seen Eddie?" was the question before I entered the room. "Have you seen Harry?"

"He was over here at half past two; he and Eddie went over to Josie Gray's. I think—"

What she thought I never knew, for at that moment Eddie rushed in breathless, screaming, "Mother, Mother! Harry Loring is drowned! We were sliding on the millpond and there was a hole in the ice with snow on it, and Harry didn't see it, and—"

"Hush, Eddie!" said his mother, looking at me fearfully. "Here is Mrs. Loring."

There was a great silence in the room, broken only by the blithe, sweet voice of a canary, and a purr of a Maltese cat. Presently Mrs. Potter came toward me, and placed her hand softly upon my shoulder saying, "Ella, my poor child!"

I never moved, but sat with wide open eyes upon an awful picture. A cold, gray afternoon, a pond, little boys playing upon it, one little figure well known to me, suddenly disappearing through the treacherous ice—down, down, the little hands grasping at cruel weeds, the sweet mouth full of water. And those wicked, sinful words ringing through my ears, "I don't care where you go, as long as you keep out of my sight." There was a mist before my eyes, a ringing in my ears; I remember leaving the house with a blind feeling of going where my Harry was. Then came a horrible sense of the earth giving way under my feet, and I knew no more.

A pleasant feeling of warmth—a languid sense was pervading my system. I opened my eyes and glanced around the room. A strange woman was by the fire; at the foot of the bed was my husband with his hand over his eyes. I tried to think where I was, and what had happened, but in vain. Then my attention was arrested by a little figure in a red flannel night dress, cuddled up in a big chair—my Harry! Then it all flashed across my mind. I sat up straight in bed with a faint "Why!"

"What is it?" said I, feebly.

"You must not talk; lie down. Oh, darling, darling?" and the strong man wept like a child. And the little figure came and jumped on my bed and, putting his arms around my neck, cried, too. And I, puzzled to know what it all meant, cried also. The strange figure came forward and took Harry away, saying, "Be careful, Mr. Loring, everything now depends upon quiet."

"Tell me now," said I. "I must know! I had such a terrible feeling. Oh, Harold; I dreamed that Harry was drowned!"

His face grew white. "He was near death; George Gray got him out of the pond; Gray sent down to the office for me; I went after Dr. Hooper and came right up. There was but a spark of life left, but we succeeded at last."

"How many days ago was it, Harold?" I asked.

"Seven weeks ago yesterday," said he smiling.

"Seven weeks!" said I. "Impossible!"

"You have been very sick with brain fever, Ella. You were very near death; for days we despaired of ever seeing you conscious again. You would say, 'Harry is drowned, and I made him drown himself.' Last night Dr. Hooper said the crisis was at hand; if you lived through the night you would get well. Oh, Ella! I am so thankful you were spared to me!"

"I have been so weak and sinful, Harold," said I, and then told him all, not keeping back anything.

He heard me through, stroking my hair in a gentle fashion. When I finished he said, "It has taught you a lesson, Ella dear." And that was all.

I soon recovered. For a long time I could not bear Harry out of my sight. It seemed as if I could not do enough to atone for my wicked conduct. The thought makes me shudder now—if it had been that Harry had not come back to me and that the last words he heard from his mother's lips were so unkind. I have had three children since then, and not one of them has heard a cross or hasty word from me. Oftentimes my patience is sorely tired, but one thought of that horrible death to which Harry came so near drives the demon away.

Mothers, bear patiently with these innocent little ones. Are there not many whose eyes resting on this simple story fill with bitter tears at the recollection of the unkind words, and even blows, to little children laid away forever, who would give all their worldly possessions, yes, years of their lives, to recall those hasty words that made their child's lips quiver pitifully and the clear eyes dim with tears? Ah! You cannot have them back even for a moment to kiss the sweet, red lips. They are gone, and *your sin* remains.

Angry Words

"Let's play visiting," said Jennie. "You be Uncle John, and I'll be Mother, and I'll come and make you a visit."

"Pshaw!" said Dick, scornfully; "that's girls' play, and it's silly. Let's play soldier, that's ever so much better!"

"It isn't a bit more silly than soldier is, and not half as hard work. I won't play it, anyway," and Jennie sat down on the steps very determinedly.

"You're real mean!" cried Dick, impetuously, "and I know you're lazy or you wouldn't say playing soldier is hard work. I'd like to play it all day. Come now, won't you?"

"Oh, Dick, I can't," said Jennie, pushing her hair out of her eyes, "it's so warm, and I'm so tired."

"Tired! Pooh! Lazy you mean!" Dick said, with a contemptuous sneer.

"I'm not lazy," protested Jennie, "not a bit more than you are."

"Then come and play," said Dick.

"I'll play visiting," said Jennie, "but I won't play soldier."

Dick's temper was up.

"You ugly, good-for-nothing girl. I'll never play with you again! I hate you! There now! And I wish you'd never speak to me again so long as you live!"

Dick did not stop to think what he was saying. His anger was so fierce and deep that he could not check it, and it poured itself out in a torrent of bitter words. Did I say he could not check it? Perhaps he might have done so, but he did not try.

"I don't care what you say," answered Jennie, very coolly. "I won't play soldier anyway," she added, with a laugh at Dick's red face and angry gestures.

Dick did not answer back, for he was too mad to speak, and Jennie got up and went into the house, leaving him alone. Shortly after, Mrs. Grey called Dick and sent him to the village on an errand.

It was nearly dark before he got back, and his mother informed him that Jennie had gone to bed not feeling very well. So Dick did not see her again that day. The next morning he was told that she was very sick. She had taken ill suddenly, and the doctor had been sent for in the night. He came and pronounced it a very bad case of fever.

Poor Dick! The very first thought that entered his mind was—what if Jennie should die? And then the memory of his cruel, wicked words came up before him, and he felt ashamed of himself. Somehow he could not get the thought out of his mind that if she should die he should feel guilty all his life. How much he would have given to unsay those words. But there was no way in which he could get them out of his mind. They haunted him continually.

Day by day Jennie grew worse. Dick plead to be allowed to see her for just one moment, but the doctor would not allow it. Strict quiet was ordered, and none but her parents were admitted in the sick room. It seemed to Dick that he could not possibly get along a great while without asking her forgiveness. He could think of nothing but his unkindness. It seemed so strange that he could ever use such words to her, his only sister!

At last the doctor said there was no hope for Jennie. She would die in spite of all he could do for her. When Dick heard this, he made up his mind that he must see her again. He did not see how he could stand it if she were to die and not tell him that she forgave him for being so unkind and saying such bad, cruel things. He remembered how she had complained of feeling tired, and he knew she must have felt the approach of the disease that now had her in its clasp. And he had called her "lazy" when she was sick!

How still the room was where Jennie lay. He was not refused when he asked to see her once more. There was no need of his being kept away any longer, for the disease had gone too far to admit of hope Dr. Thorne had said.

Dick stood by the bed and looked down into the poor, pale face of his little sister. Great tears welled up into his eyes and dropped over his cheeks like rain, when he saw the change a week had wrought.

"Oh, Jennie, say you forgive me before you die! Please, do, Jennie, for I can't bear it any longer so," Dick cried and knelt down by the bedside with his face close to hers.

"I love you Dick," she replied in a faint, weak voice, and held up her lips for a kiss. Dick kissed her with such a pang at his heart! How he would miss her when she was gone!

Jennie closed her eyes wearily. They thought she was dying, and the doctor lifted Dick up gently from the bed. But it was not death; after a little she opened her eyes again, and then with a sweet, touching smile said she was going to sleep. And she did sleep, not the last, long sleep of death, as they imagined it to be, but slumber quiet and refreshing. When she awoke from it, the doctor said she would recover if nothing happened to prevent it more than he could foresee. Her disease had turned, and Jennie had a chance for her life after all.

And she did get well. Dick was her most faithful nurse. The lesson he had learned was never forgotten, and he never afterward let his anger get the control of his better judgment.

Guard Well Thy Lips

Guard well thy lips; none, none can know
What evils from the tongue may flow;
What guilt, what grief, may be incurred,
By one incautious, hasty word.

Be "slow to speak"; look well within,
To check what there may lead to sin;
And pray unceasingly for aid,
Lest unawares thou be betrayed.

"Condemn not, judge not"—not to man
Is given his bother's faults to scan;
One task is thine, and one alone,
To search out and subdue thine own.

Indulge no murmurings; oh, restrain
Those lips so ready to complain!
Let words of wisdom, meekness, love,
Thy heart's true renovation prove.

Set God before thee; every word
Thy lips pronounce by Him is heard;

Oh, couldst thou realize this thought,
What care, what caution, would be taught!

Think on thy parting hour; ere long
The approach of death may chain thy tongue,
And powerless all attempts be found,
To articulate one meaning sound.

"The time is short"—this day may be
The very last assigned to thee;
So speak, that shouldst thou ne'er speak more,
Thou mayest not this day's words deplore.

Flossy and His Mistress

"Oh, you dear little Flossy!" said Miss Adelia, picking up her sky terrier, "nobody has given you a crumb today nor brushed out your pretty curls. You are always neglected when Adelia is away. But you shall not be any more, pretty pet. She will take you with her next time she makes a visit. Oh! Run away, Freddy, don't plague me with your lesson. I must go down and broil a mutton chop for Flossy; the little dear is almost starved."

So she pushed away her little brother and made Flossy a snug bed on the sofa cushion, patting him softly as she left him. She then went down to the kitchen to burn her fingers and disarrange Bridget's tidy apartment, in the preparation of a breakfast fit for her "treasure." Miss Adelia would have considered herself most unjustly treated if she had been obliged to take half the trouble for the accommodation of anyone else in the family, but for her Flossy she could do anything. Just in proportion as her attachment for this senseless creature increased, her regard for everything else appeared to diminish. She grew cross and fretful when asked to perform the simplest service for anyone. But she could spend hours over her dog, bathing him, curling his hair in little rings, and sprinkling him with fragrant perfume. The pet endured it as well as he could but would have been a far happier dog if he had been permitted to pick his bones in the courtyard and go to sleep in the sun.

"Oh, Mother, I can't take the tiresome baby; he is so cross. I never could endure a baby just big enough to tear everything to atoms. Besides, I want to curl up poor Flossy; he looks as shaggy as a street dog."

"I wish he were a street dog with all my heart," said her mother. "It was a very unlucky thing for us all when your cousin made you the present of that dog. It takes up altogether too much of your time and is making you very selfish, my child. Your father and I have decided that, unless you make a decided change in the matter, Flossy must be disposed of."

"Send away poor Flossy? Oh, Mother," and Adelia burst into tears as she spoke. "Don't you know, Mother, he is worth his weight in silver. Cousin Charley said some of these terriers are worth their weight in gold. A gentleman refused a thousand-dollar span of horses for a pair he owned."

"I think the old Quaker's remark on a parallel case would hold good then, that two fools met that time—one to make such an offer, and the other to refuse it. Pets are very well in their place, but when they take up so much time and attention they become a positive injury. It is always a pleasant sight to me to go into old Margaret's little cottage and see her great tortoise-shell cat purring away so contentedly on the hearth rug, for I know how much company she is for the lonely woman. But poor Miss Hobson exposes herself to a great deal of ridicule by her attachment to her poll parrot. You know how much time she spends over him, trying to teach him new words, talking with him, and petting him like a spoiled child. It makes her seem very silly to other people who have far more important pursuits in life than tending a bird. I understand that she has bequeathed him a thousand dollars in her will and a hundred dollars a year to a person who is to take care of him after her death. So it will be for the woman's interest to prolong his life as long as possible. The poor lady is very ill now, but screeching Polly is seldom out of her room; she seems unhappy if he is out of her sight. Now, if Miss Hobson had only taken into her home and heart some poor motherless child years ago, what a blessing it might be to her now! Instead of being dependent for every comfort on hirelings, she might have a child's loving attentions in her old age.

"God never intended us to lavish so much time and attention upon a mere animal. He wishes us to be kind to even the humblest of his creatures, but He has given everyone a higher work to do than curling and perfuming a dog. I have observed with great anxiety and pain how this attachment is growing upon you and how it is injuring your mind and heart; and now, Adelia, you must give up devoting so much time to it, or I shall give Flossy away to anyone who will take him. It would be better, indeed, to have him killed, than to have him the means of making my daughter selfish and ridiculous. You may think of this seriously, Adelia, and tomorrow morning you may tell me your decision. If you think you can keep him and not have him interfere with one other duty, you may do so. Another thing I shall insist on. There are to be no more meals cooked expressly for him. It took Bridget half an hour to clean up after your breakfast-making this morning, and that must not occur again. He can eat scraps from the table like any other dog, or he cannot stay with us."

"Oh, Mother," said Adelia, "I cannot think what Henrietta Bradshaw will say to that. She always cooks something nice for her King Charles and feeds him on a china plate."

"Is it to imitate Henrietta you have been led into all this folly, my dear?" asked her mother, smiling. "I thought it was pure affection for your pet. But here comes Aunt Sophia; perhaps she can help us solve the knotty question of what shall be done with Flossy."

Aunt Sophia listened to the account of the matter, and at length proposed to take Flossy to board. Not that she was particularly fond of pets, but she was anxious that so fine a girl her niece might make, should not be spoiled for a little terrier dog no bigger than your fist.

As school commenced the next week, Adelia at length consented to the arrangement. It would be a good excuse to offer to Miss Henrietta, and it would sound well, too, to say that she had sent him to the country to board for a while.

Floss seemed to enjoy the country air and romped and frolicked with the kittens just as any plebeian puppy might have done, but one day he fell into a fit. It did not last long, however, yet Aunt Sophia thought it of enough importance to mention when she came to town one day with her butter.

"Oh, Auntie, do get the doctor for him if it ever happens again. He lives just next door to you, so it would not be a bit of trouble. Henrietta often has Dr. Allen look at her King Charles when he does not seem as well as usual. Once he gave him some medicine in a little vial, which Henrietta had the hardest work to get him to take. I suppose it was very bitter, for Charley did make such a face, and cry, and rub his nose. Dr. Allen, and Henrietta's sister Laura sat on the sofa laughing till they cried, and poor Hetty cried, too, for the poor dog's sufferings."

"By all means get Dr. King to attend Floss if he needs it," said Father, who began to see a glimmering hope of someday getting clear of "the plague." "I will write a line to him I think."

Adelia almost thought her father was jesting, but he did send a line by Aunt Sophia. It might not have added to her happiness if she had seen its contents, however.

Perhaps the doctor had attended ladies' lapdogs before. At least he made no hesitation in pouring a little crystallized powder down his throat, which soon relieved him of all the ills of his life.

Aunt Sophia sent in a line to say that poor Flossy was dead, and the children had buried him at the foot of the apple tree. There were a good many tears shed that evening by one member of the family, and Adelia thought her father quite hardhearted to turn to his newspaper with so much interest, right after she had told him of her affliction. She wished to run over at once to her friend Henrietta for consolation, and her mother permitted her to go for a while. She found that young lady deeply immersed in dress-fitting anxieties; her dressmakers were happening not to please her, so she had no eyes or ears for her friend's sorrows. She listened with the greatest indifference to her account of poor Flossy's untimely end, and only offered the consoling remark, "It was only what you might have expected, sending him away from home, and trusting him to the care of another. I never permit anyone else to have the charge of my little darling," and she stopped in the midst of her employment to give him a caress.

Adelia speedily drew her visit to a close and when she returned was ready to accompany her mother on a walk. She began to realize the truth which her mother had sought to impress upon her, that mere fashionable friendships were very unsubstantial affairs. They were worth but little at times when we felt we needed them most.

But where was her mother taking her? This was a portion of town she had never visited before. She almost shrank back with dismay from the narrow alley they entered, where they were obliged to pick their way very carefully through the rubbish which littered the sidewalk. But her mother knew the way and stopped at last before a crumbling doorway, which Adelia almost feared to enter.

Knocking softly at a door, it was speedily opened, and the two entered an apartment which, with all its poverty, was a pleasant contrast to all without. The bare walls were whitewashed, and the floor was clean, and so was the little pallet in the corner where lay a form as white as the little dress it wore. A bowed and heartbroken mother went back to her station at the foot of the little bed as soon as her guests were seated. No word could she utter, but she folded back the white covering from the little waxen from, and then her sobs and moans broke forth afresh. Adelia's ready tears flowed forth in sympathy, and her mother's eyes were dim even while she gently strove to lift the poor woman's thoughts up to that blessed land where Jesus will gather all the tender lambs into His bosom.

"I know, ma'am, it is much better for her, the beautiful rosebud; but, oh! The weary nights and days for me that's to come. She'll never nestle up to her poor mother's bosom in the dark night again, when the noises in the house and street frighten her. Poor lamb! I was forced to leave her the day she was taken sick to take home some work to a lady. She kept me waiting in the hall for an hour before I could see her, and then, ma'am, she would give me no money. 'She hadn't it by her,' she said, 'and I must call again.' O ma'am, it made my blood run cold in me to hear her say that. She, with her wealth and plenty, didn't know what a deathstroke it was to me, with my darling sick, and me not a penny to buy her a sup of milk, or a thing to refresh her. I came back to the room, though I was blind and dizzy with famine, but I could have found my child, I believe, if I had been blindfolded. I carried her up and down the room, rocked her in my arms till she fell asleep, and then I stole out with my shawl on my arm to the pawnbroker's shop. It was the last thing I had that was worth their looking at, and it brought me enough to buy some things for her and a stale loaf for myself. There's some of it left there still. It seems as if I could never taste food again. But I must make haste with my work, or I shall not get the money to pay for my baby's burial, and I can't bear to see her rattled off over the stones in a pine coffin like a poor beggar child."

She reached out her hand and took up a paper which contained her work, a beautiful piece of braiding on a jacket of violet merino.

"Why, that is just like Henrietta Bradshaw's new dress," said Adelia. "She has it made with a jacket just like that, and it was to be braided in just such a pattern. We selected it from a magazine."

"It is for that same young lady, Miss, and I only hope I may please her—though she might have let me wait when my baby lay dead in the house," she said, almost bitterly.

"Oh, Henrietta will not ask you to do it now!" said Adelia earnestly. "She could not do such a thing. I am sure she would pay you beforehand and allow you to finish it afterward."

"If she will pay me when it is done, Miss, I shall be thankful; but it was of her I begged the money that was due me, so I could buy food for my dying child but it was refused me."

It seemed incredible to the warm-hearted Adelia that anyone could be so hard-hearted; but she did not reflect how rapidly she was drifting in the same direction. After her mother had given the woman a sum sufficient for the present necessity and left the contents of the little basket she carried, she took Adelia's hand and walked away toward their own pleasant home again. Oh, how different the world seemed when they were out once more in the broad sunny street, away from that dismal alley! Yet Adelia's thoughts went constantly back to the poor woman alone with her great sorrow. There was no escape into the bright sunshine of life again.

"Oh, Mother, I do not know how she can bear it," she said at last.

"This is one of the real sorrows of life, my child. There is nothing like meeting such grief as this face-to-face to cure us of a great many fanciful sorrows."

"You will never see me cry for Flossy again, Mother. It may do very well for a plaything, but I see it was nothing to love and mourn for, when there are such sorrows as this in the world."

The mother's heart rose up in a prayer of thanksgiving to find that the lesson she had sought to teach had been learned; and she also prayed that it might be lasting.

"But can Henrietta know the truth of the case, Mother, and yet insist on having her work done at once?"

"I suppose she does not realize the poor mother's grief as you do, Adelia. But when the heart is so given up to the frivolities of fashion and the love of what should be only an occasional diversion, it grows hard very fast. Can you not realize that, my dear?"

Adelia blushed and held down her head, for she remembered how pettish she had grown of late when the baby or little Fred required her attention. She thought, with a shiver, what it would be to see those little meddlesome fingers, that often tried her so, lying cold and waxen white like those of the little one she had just left. In her heart she felt that she could never be so impatient with them again.

The lesson which she learned in that dreary alley was one of lifelong service to her. From that hour she took a more intelligent interest in the sorrows and sufferings of the poor and needy and even learned to deny herself that she might relieve their wants. She had, it is true, a succession of pets and was seldom without one. Mother was glad to see these marks of a tender and loving spirit toward the little creatures God had given to be with us, but she never again permitted one to steal away the time and service which belonged to parents, brothers, and friends, or to the Lord's poor and suffering ones.

Sowing

Who are sowing? Who are sowing?
These young children now at play;
And the scattered seeds are growing,
Night by night and day by day;
Some with fruitful grain are shooting;
Some will only weeds produce,
Which, alas, will need uprooting,
Ere the soil be fit for use.

Who are sowing? Those just leaving
Childhood and its sports behind;
Hearts with golden visions heaving,
Are they sowing to the wind?
If they toil, on Christ relying;
If His glory be their aim;
They may hope, with hope undying,
They shall reap immortal fame.

The Orphans

Moving slowly along Prince Street one afternoon, I heard the measured tramp of numerous little feet behind me. Turning around, I saw that this sound proceeded from about a hundred boys and girls belonging to one of the charitable institutions. It was a pleasing sight to see these children appear happy. They had the hue of good health on their countenances, their dress was plain, but comfortable and clean; no fantastic grotesquely cut clothes disfigured their little persons, nor did they wear any badge to tell the world that they were children of misfortune.

I entered into the conversation with one of the teachers, who informed me that they were going to view the Zoological Gardens, and that, with such a prospect before them, they were quite delighted. The little troop passed up St. Andrew Street, and as I was going in the same direction, I moved along in the front, conversing with one of the boys—the girls being all behind. Passing down St. Andrew Street south, my attention was directed to two boys about fourteen years of age. Each was driving a small pony, attached to a cart. The first boy, when he saw the children, called out to his young friend who was a little behind, and the moment his eye caught the sight he leaped from the cart with a spring, crying out, "James, I'll see my sister! I'll see my little sister!" He drew his horse quickly to the side of the pavement, and left it alone the instant the girls came toward him. Just as he commenced his anxious search, his horse moved off. He sprung to its head and checked its progress, and in an instant he was at the front ranks of the girls, keenly glancing along the line to discover his little sister. Being all dressed alike, it was not easy to distinguish any one in particular without the strictest search.

On they passed, but his sister came not. Poor boy, thought I, his kind heart will be doomed to suffer disappointment as his little sister does not appear to be among them, and from his sorrowful look, he thought so too. They all passed but two—his sister was one of them. The anxious boy rushed to her, and grasping one of her hands in his, he placed his other gently on her neck, and could only say, "Mary." The little girl, who appeared to be about seven years of age, looked up, and oh, such ecstasy! She was by the side of her brother. She clasped her little arms around him, and her sweet face was lighted up with smiles. He bowed down his head to catch the few hurried words she spoke to him, and let her hear his little tale. He took his eyes from off her face but once, and only once, and that for a moment, and this was to see that his pony was still where he left it. The poor brute seemed to be sensible of the sacred mission on which its conductor had gone, as it moved not. He again bowed down his head to breathe into the ear of his beloved and loving sister his few parting words, for he could not go any farther; they grasped each other's hands and exchanged looks of tenderness, and the little girl moved on with her companions. His eyes saw nothing but that one loved object; they followed her along. The children in front turned down York Place, and before she was out of her brother's view, she turned round, and with a smile, held out her hand in token of adieu. The boy started as her face met his gaze and moving one step forward held out both his hands—the next moment she was hid from his sight.

He slowly returned toward his horse, and while a tear moistened his eye and a cast of melancholy shrouded his countenance, there was something like an expression of satisfaction and pleasure on his features. He mounted his little cart, and, as I turned from beholding this affecting scene, there was a dimness over my eyes which took a few applications of my handkerchief to remove.

This was food for reflection. I thought on the thousands who never knew what it was to want the fostering care of a mother, or the anxious solicitude of a father; again upon the thousands who are thrown upon the charity of strangers—friendless and alone. These two young creatures, perhaps spent their first years under one roof and slept in each other's arms.

The one is now earning his bread humbly but honestly; while the other is enjoying the benefits of an excellent institution. Their meetings are few but sweet, and, as in the present case, doubly so. May the remembrance of their present lonely situation endear them more firmly to each other; and if the world should smile upon them, may they consecrate a portion of their means toward the support of those institutions which shelter and protect the orphan child.

"Girls, Help Father"

"My hands are so stiff I can hardly hold a pen," said Farmer Wilbur as he sat down to "figure out" some accounts that were getting behindhand.

"Can I help you, Father?" said Lucy, laying down her bright crochet work. "I shall be glad to do so if you will explain what you want."

"Well, I shouldn't wonder if you could, Lucy," he said reflectively. "Pretty good at figures are you?"

"It would be said if I did not know something of them, after going twice through the arithmetic," said Lucy, laughing.

"Well, I can show you, in five minutes what I have to do, and it'll be a wonderful help if you can do it for me. I never was a master hand at accounts in my best days, and it does not grow any easier since I put on spectacles."

Very patiently did the helpful daughter plod through the long lines of figures, leaving the gay worsted to lie idle all the evening, though she was in such haste to finish her scarf. It was reward enough to see her tired father, who had been toiling all day for herself and dear ones, sitting so cozily in his easy chair, enjoying his weekly paper.

The clock struck nine before her task was over, but the hearty—"Thank you, daughter, a thousand times," took away all sense of weariness.

"It's rather looking up, where a man can have such an amanuensis," said the father. "It's not every farmer that can afford it."

"Not every farmer's daughter is capable of making one," said the mother, with a little pardonable maternal pride.

"Nor everyone that would be willing, if able," said Mr. Wilbur, which last was sad truth. How many daughters might be of use to their fathers in this and many other ways, who never think of lightening a care or labor. If asked to perform some little service, it is done at best with a reluctant step and unwilling air that robs it of all sunshine or claim to gratitude.

Girls, help your father! Give him a cheerful home to rest in when evening comes, and do not worry his life away by fretting because he cannot afford you all the luxuries you covet. Children exert as great an influence on their parents as parents do on their children.

Don't Let Mother Do It!

Daughter, don't let mother do it!
  Do not let her slave and toil,
While you sit, a useless idler,
  Fearing your soft hands to soil.
Don't you see the heavy burdens
  Daily she is wont to bear,
Bring the lines upon her forehead—
  Sprinkle silver in her hair?

Daughter, don't let mother do it!
  She has cared for you so long,
Is it right the weak and feeble
  Should be toiling for the strong?
Waken from your listless languor,
  Seek her side to cheer and bless;
And your grief will be less bitter
  When the sods above her press.

Daughter, don't let mother do it!
  You will never, never know
What were home without a mother
  Till that mother lieth low—

Low beneath the budding daisies,
 Free from earthly care or pain—
To the home so sad without her,
 Never to return again.

May and Might

"Oh!" thought Anna Markham to herself as she closed the book she had been reading, a history of the mission in Madagascar, "How I wish it were possible for me to do something like this for Christ," and here Anna lost herself in a sort of heroic dream. She pictured herself teaching, exhorting the heathen in India, or in some far African station, where the gospel had never before been heard. She thought of herself as parting, almost without a regret from her friends, to encounter all the hardships of a mission life—the dangers of fever, wild beasts and persecution, especially persecution. Anna fancied herself enduring suffering, starvation, imprisonment and torture for her faith, and had just come so far in her romance as to be "led out for execution," and "forgive her murderers with her last breath," when her mother called her from the next room.

The rapt ecstatic look on Anna's face gave way instantly to a fretful frown. "Oh, *dear!*" she said sharply to herself, "I never *can* be let alone a minute."

She threw down the book and went to her mother.

"Well, what is it?" she said in a most ungracious tone.

"I want you to run over to Mrs. O'Hara and take her the dinner Katy has got ready for her, and Ann, if you can, get her up and make up her bed."

"Oh, Mother!" said Anna, as if she had been asked to perform impossibilities, "I can't bear to go to Mrs. O'Hara's, and the house is so dirty and disagreeable."

"She is an old lady and all alone," said her mother in some displeasure. "She cannot do anything for herself now, and it is the duty of her neighbors to take care of her till she is well."

"She might go to the hospital and let the Sisters of Charity take care of her."

"She won't go, as you know very well, and there are some good reasons on her side too. Besides do you think it would be any more agreeable for the Sisters to nurse Mrs. O'Hara than it is for you?"

"Well I don't like to," said Anna very crossly.

"I'll go, Aunt Jane," said Anna's cousin, Miss Kent, who was drawing by the window.

"No, Milly, Anna will go," said Mrs. Markham. "I advise you to think what manner of spirit you are of, my daughter."

Anna made no answer and she obeyed her mother, for she knew she must; but she performed her errand in so ungracious and uncharitable a manner and assumed such an air of martyrdom, that Mrs. O'Hara, who was by no means reserved in speech, told her rather decidedly that she'd "never be the lady her mother was." So Anna went home disgusted and wished herself away from a home where "no one understood her."

By the next day, however, she had forgotten about the matter and was talking to her cousin Milly about the missionary work of the church. "Oh," she said with enthusiasm, "I should like nothing better than to go as a missionary to Africa."

"What would you do there?" asked Milly, rather amused.

"Oh! Teach the children, and the women, and take care of the sick, and so forth."

"You think the heathen savages of Africa would be less disagreeable than Mrs. O'Hara and you would take more pleasure in doing for them than for your own neighbor?" asked Milly.

Anna was very much vexed for a moment, but then she began to feel a little ashamed.

"Isn't it rather better on the whole," said Milly, "to look about us and see what little things we can do if we will, than to spend the time fancying what great things we would do if we only could?"

After a little consideration, Anna began to see how little of the true missionary spirit she possessed and to feel that she was not actuated by right motives.

Nothing is more natural than for us to be selfish and love our own ways, but a feeling that would lead us to be unmindful of the fact that others have equal rights and desires for enjoyment with ourselves is a selfishness that should be overcome.

We must be willing to take up the little crosses that lie in our pathway and to labor for the good of others. In doing this we may show a true missionary spirit.

Outward Appearance

"Oh, Mattie, come down and see what a queer looking object is coming up the road!"

"Where, George, where?" echoed a chorus of voices as their owners rushed pell-mell to the open window and protruded their several heads therefrom, while eager eyes scanned the road in search of the curious object to which George had called his sister's attention.

"Why, there, up the road; wait a moment; she's gone down in the hollow. You'll see her directly coming over the brow of that hill there, right opposite father's meadow."

"Is it a person, George?" inquired Mattie, turning her bright, blue eyes in the direction indicated.

"Why, yes, it is a woman to be sure, but the funniest one it was ever my fortune to see. There, there she comes, the very queen of witches."

All eyes were fastened upon the figure which now appeared in sight and proved to be a woman apparently well advanced in years, if one might judge by the bent form and slow, cautious step with which she advanced. The dark gray cloak in which she was enveloped seemed to be of some ancient style and designed for extremely cold climates, since it consisted of numerous capes, each surmounting the other—the whole combination imparting to the wearer a very bunchy appearance, which, to say the least, was exceedingly grotesque. Her bonnet was huge in dimensions, such as were worn years ago by our grandmothers. In one hand she carried a cotton umbrella, though the day was exceedingly fine, while in the other she held what appeared to be a box or large square parcel, securely covered with a newspaper. On one arm hung an old-fashioned reticule filled to its utmost capacity. As she arrived opposite the house she paused and carefully depositing her large package on the ground, glanced uneasily up and down the road as if uncertain which way to proceed. From some receptacle beneath the huge proportions of her cloak she drew forth a palm-leaf fan and proceeded to avail herself of its cooling properties, thereby proving herself provided with comforts peculiar to either cold or warm weather. The little group at the windows watched her with considerable interest.

"Poor creature," said Mattie, "I dare say she is tired; I am sure she has walked a great way today."

"Then why don't she sit down on that great box and rest a while?" responded George.

"Perhaps she can't—maybe it's a bandbox."

"Sure enough, that's a wise suggestion. I've no doubt that's just the truth of the matter; no woman travels without a bandbox, even if she does go on foot.

How is this—why, if the funny old creature isn't coming here!" And sure enough she had again taken up her baggage and, to their utter amazement, was slowly walking down the lane leading to the house.

"She has probably lost her way and is coming to inquire about the roads," suggested George.

"That can't be," said Walter Jones, one of George's playmates, who had been an amused spectator of the old lady's proceedings. "While you were discussing the bandbox question, Farmer Colby passed by, and the old woman stopped him and seemed to be inquiring about someone. He listened a moment and then pointed over here, and she started at once in this direction. I congratulate you, George, on your new acquaintance, possibly some maiden aunt from the backwoods, of whose existence you have never been informed."

Having delivered this speech he laughed so tauntingly that George colored deeply as he replied with spirit, "We haven't got any such relations, Walter Jones; our connections are all people of respectability."

"George Grey—come, now, that's rich; can't an odd-looking old woman be respectable?"

"Have a care what you say, sir; I don't know anything about her or any other backwoods people."

"Nobody said you did, that I am aware of."

"Pshaw, George, what's the use of quarreling about a poor old woman, just because she looks funny?" said Mattie. "I'm going down to see what she wants." And with a light step she bounded down the stairs.

"Come on, George," said Walter, "we won't quarrel about her; let us go down, too, and see what she looks like on closer inspection."

They arrived in the hall just in time to see Mrs. Grey seize the old lady's hands in hers as with an expression of pleasure as she drew her into the cozy family sitting room and closed the door.

"There," exclaimed Walter, triumphantly, "didn't I tell you it was your aunt come to see you! Come, now, why don't you go in and welcome her to Greyside Villa?"

"Nonsense, Walter Jones, I tell you she is no relation of mine."

"Ah! How do you know that? I'm sure she was very cordially welcomed by your mother."

"My mother is always very kind to everyone. If the old lady called on any charitable mission for others, or was in want of assistance herself, my mother would treat her well."

"But does she take every beggar or peddler by both hands and express delight at seeing them? Does she lead them into her pleasant sitting room in that agreeable style? If she does, I wonder that Greyside Villa is not daily besieged by objects of charity from all parts of the country."

The discussion was here cut short by the appearance of Mrs. Grey in the hall, accompanied by her strange visitor. They proceeded up the stairs together and had scarcely reached the landing above, when Walter gave vent to a shout of laughter, exclaiming, "What an acquisition to Greyside Villa! Three cheers for the queen of witches!"

George was evidently annoyed but made no reply to the rude speech. Mattie was ready to cry with vexation as Walter, with a boy's love of teasing, turned to her saying, "She has come to stay a week, Mattie, at all events, perhaps longer. I'm going home to send Mother over to call on her. I'm sure she'd be delighted to make her acquaintance and learn how affairs are progressing in the backwoods." So saying, he strode away, whistling a favorite air.

After a little while Mrs. Grey came down alone and called George and Mattie into the sitting room. "My children," said she, "I was grieved to hear you speak so disrespectfully of any aged person as you did of the old lady who is now my guest."

"Why, Mother," said George, "we didn't know she was coming here; and if I did call her the queen of witches, I didn't mean any disrespect to her really. I'm sure, Mother, you must admit she's very odd-looking, but do tell us, who is she?"

"It was Walter Jones that laughed so loud, Mother," put in Mattie, with the evident desire of clearing her brother.

"Yes, Mother, he said she was my aunt from the backwoods and made all manner of sport of what he chose to call my new relation."

"And Mother," exclaimed Mattie, "he said he was going home to send his mother over to call on her, and you know they are such awful proud people," and Mattie looked exceedingly grave, as she delivered this important piece of news.

"I would be glad to see my children pay due respect to age, no matter what the surrounding circumstances may be. Appearances are often deceitful, and the roughest exterior frequently conceals the warmest heart and most lovable character. Sit down by me here in the twilight, and I will tell you something of the history of the old lady in question while she is resting upstairs. Left an orphan at an early age, she was taken to the home of an uncle who soon became weary of the charge and proved unfaithful to his trust. She was treated very unkindly and made to feel her dependence in every possible way. She never had the pleasure of looking back upon the joys of childhood, since to her there was nothing but trouble and care. Her married life was for a time a happy period, but even this path was not devoid of thorns. Her husband was killed by a steamboat accident while on his way home from a distant city, and she was not even able to recover his remains. She was left alone with the care of three small children, two of whom fell victim to an epidemic which was prevalent at that time.

"The eldest son was spared, and no mother was ever blessed with a nobler boy than Willie Cramer. But the time came when even this was to be taken from her. You remember, my son, the terrible times through which we passed a few years ago, when our country was in danger, and the true, loyal hearts of her brave sons interposed themselves between her and ruin. Regiment after regiment went forward, and still the call came for more men. Brave, truehearted Willie Cramer went about his daily duties with downcast looks; he seldom spoke of the war yet was always eager for the latest news. One evening as Mrs. Cramer passed his room, the door of which was slightly ajar, she heard him praying and stood riveted to the spot as his words fell upon her ears. He was asking God to direct him in the matter which pressed so heavily upon his heart; he prayed that if it was right for him to go forth in defense of his country, that God would put it into the heart of his mother to consent to his going. Mrs. Cramer pondered over the subject a long time. She wept and prayed and finally called her son to her side and frankly asked him if he really wished to leave her for his country's sake.

"'Mother,' said he, 'if I could go with your free consent, if I could feel that you willingly gave me to our country's cause, with your blessing upon my head, I would gladly go, but without this I cannot leave you.'

"It was a terrible struggle for Mrs. Cramer. At least self was subdued. One evening as Willie stood on the little rustic porch, listening to the sounds of martial music from the distance, his mother came and stood beside him. Placing her trembling hand upon his head, she said, 'Willie, my son, go, and God be with you always; your mother's blessing and prayers shall follow you wherever you are.' And so Willie Cramer, young, but so noble and brave, joined a company then forming in the neighborhood and was soon far away fighting the battles of his country. The first year passed. One sad day the news came that the bright, noble boy was with the slain. When Mrs. Cramer rallied from the blow she felt that henceforth life was nothing to her, only as she could use it in the service of others. She accordingly went to the hospital as a nurse, and a more faithful, tender one was never known. It was she who so faithfully watched beside your father there, when he lay so long with that terrible fever brought on by exposure. It was she who wrote me every day or two to relieve my anxiety when my own illness prevented me from going to him myself. Never, my children can your father forget how kind she was to him and how much we owe to her for his restoration to health. After the close of the war, she returned to her native place and has spent her time in doing good. When the epidemic broke out in the city of M., she hastened hither to care for the sick, pray with the dying, and comfort the bereaved. Having occasion to come to our neighborhood on a mission of mercy, she felt a desire to see the dear children of whom your father talked so much during his long illness. The moment her name was announced I hastened to welcome her, glad, indeed, to do honor to one who has done so much for us. And now, bowed down more by toil, care, and trouble than by the weight of years, and though she is odd-looking, though she does adhere to the same style of dress, notwithstanding the changes of fashion, does it make her any less the truehearted, self-sacrificing woman she has proved herself to be? Can you wonder that I was pained by your ill-timed mirth? Oh! I do trust, my dear children, that in the future you will never fail to show respect to age, no matter what the surrounding circumstances and never trust mere outward appearance as the only credentials of character and standing."

You may be sure George and Mattie were both heartily ashamed of the part they had acted. George colored deeply when the newspaper was removed from the singular-looking package, and it proved to be a cage containing a pair of beautiful birds, a present for himself, which kind Mrs. Cramer had brought, though it must have been a source of discomfort and trouble to herself to carry. The well-filled reticule which had caused such merriment contained a doll for baby Lillian, the household pet, several books, and a workbox all complete for Mattie. Anxious to make amends, they both endeavored to interest the kind old lady in every possible way, notwithstanding the scornful looks of Walter Jones. They never forgot the lesson thus learned or allowed themselves to again be governed by outward appearance.

The Cross Family

"Dear me! I think we are rightly named; for we are certainly the *crossest* family on record!" exclaimed Margaret Cross, as she threw herself on a stool and leaned her head on the windowsill. "There's mother grumbling at Tom because he whistles in the house, and father just snapped at me because I asked a favor of him. And it's just so all the time; sharp, harsh answers and cutting sarcasm are the most of our conversation with each other."

"Why don't you set the example by acting the Miss Amiable yourself, then?" retorted her sister Clara, who stood before the mirror arranging her hair.

"I should have a pleasant time of it in the way of snubs and sneers if I did," replied Margaret. "But, really, Clara, it has troubled me very much of late; in fact, ever since I visited Aunt Alice and saw such a contrast. They were all so polite to one another and so careful of one another's feelings, that it was a comfort to be with them."

"I hope you took a few lessons," remarked Clara, sneeringly, "and can instruct in the art."

"I should have a large field to labor in, but I very much fear most of it would prove to be stony soil," replied Margaret. The conversation here ended,

Clara soon left the room, and Margaret was alone with her thoughts.

"It is the truth," she said bitterly to herself. "It's the truth. We are so wrapped up in our mantles of selfishness that natural love between us is being frozen to death. Even father and mother seem to have lost all love for each other—if they ever had any and I suppose they had once—and as for us girls and Tom, why we would as soon think of flying as of waiting upon one another. And I verily believe if one of us kissed another they would think that one insane. I am so tired of this endless snapping and snarling. I mean to try to do something to make our family a more united one, and if they laugh at me they may. I'll begin this very moment. Mary has one of her hard headaches. I will go there and sit by her, if I do no more."

With a firm desire to do and a resolution to try to bring about a more perfect state of harmony, Margaret arose and went to her sister's room. She opened the door softly and walked in. Mary was lying with closed eyes and moaning as if in great pain. She opened her eyes languidly at the sound of Margaret's footsteps but closed them immediately.

Margaret softly approached the bed and laying her hand on her sister's head, said, "Poor girl! Does your head ache so? Let me bathe or rub it for you."

Mary, all unused to sympathy or assistance, replied, "No, nothing will help it. Just let me alone and it will get well itself."

"But can't I do something for you?"

"No, I don't want anything done. I've stood it so long, I guess I can stand it a little longer," replied Mary, fretfully.

If Margaret had expected to have her sympathy appreciated, this repulse might have disheartened her; but she had expected just such a greeting and had made up her mind how to act. Without noticing her sister's words, she hastened to the kitchen, procured a basin of water, and returning to her sister's side, she bound up the aching head, bathed the throbbing temples, and moistened the feverish hands. Mary made no resistance, but lay with her eyes closed, while Margaret performed these acts of kindness. Then she closed the blinds, sat down by the bedside and very soon had the satisfaction of knowing, by the quiet breathing, that Mary was asleep. Then Margaret stole softly out of the room, and a feeling of joy stole into her own heart that had never been there before. This was her first lesson in the book of sympathy, and she found it sweet as the breath of morning.

Perhaps Margaret Cross would not have been at this time of her life experimenting, as it were, in this new field, had the circumstances of her life been other than they were. But the Cross children had been born and bred in the school of self-reliance. Their mother believed that children could be very easily spoiled by too much manifested love. Hence she had disciplined them to a rigid denial of caressings and drove the wedge of selfishness in their hearts which was to make the family one scene of discord. They easily learned how much sympathy to expect from the fountain head; for if they came with a bruised body, she might bind up the wounds with rags, at the same time taking particular pains to impress upon their minds the fact that their own carelessness was the prime cause of the disaster. If they came with a bruised heart, however, sympathy cost more than rags, so was withheld. Thus it was that the Cross children grew up, "wrapped in their mantles of selfishness," as Margaret had said, until, as far as regards the inner life, they were as far apart as if a continent divided them.

"What are you doing, Margaret? Why don't you come to your dinner?" said Mrs. Cross, as the family, except Mary and Margaret, were seated at the table. "I'm coming soon, Mother, but do not wait." Presently Margaret entered with a waiter, on which was some nicely browned toast.

"Heigho!" exclaimed her brother Tom. "Queen Margaret feels dainty tonight; so do I," and reaching over, he took the brown slice. All now expected outburst. None more than Tom himself. But Margaret only looked at him with a queer expression about the mouth—a half-laugh and half-serious pucker—and said, "Well, I can make more; take it, Tom, if you wish." But Tom did not want it. He had taken it for the sole purpose of teasing her and failed. So he passed it back to her, saying, "I don't want your baby feed; I only wanted to see your eyes snap."

"Was that your game? Then you deserve a box"; and she good-naturedly slapped his ear and started for the stairway.

"Where are you going?" asked her mother, calling sharply after her.

"To Mary's room. I thought maybe she could eat something if I took it to her," answered Margaret.

"Is Mary so sick?" inquired Mr. Cross.

"I didn't know't was anything but one of her headaches," answered Mrs. Cross, anxiously.

"That's all it is, too," said Clara. "But Margaret has turned Good Samaritan. I looked into the room this afternoon, and there sat Margaret bathing Mary's head, which was all bundled up, and fanning her as if she were in the last stages. I offered to do something for her this morning, but she very coolly told me to let her alone, and so I did."

No more was said until Margaret returned, when Mrs. Cross asked if Mary was better.

"She says she is, but she is very weak. She has suffered intensely," said Margaret.

"How did she consent to let you administer to her needs?" asked Clara, raising her eyebrows and looking at Margaret. "She sent me off pretty quick when I offered *my* services."

"I didn't *offer* my services," answered Margaret.

"She did not ask them, I am sure. She would die first," said Tom.

"No, she did not ask them, nor did I ask, 'What wilt thou have me do?' There's always plenty to do if one wants to do it," said Margaret pleasantly.

"Oh, dear!" said Clara. "That's your practice, is it? Well, I am sure if one does not accept my services when I offer them *I* shall not urge the matter."

"It's my opinion that precious few have ever had the chance to refuse them," said Tom, rising from the table and preparing for his visit downtown.

"No one asked your opinion, sir," retorted Clara.

"How quick she can ruffle up," said Tom, provokingly.

"Oh, Tom!" said Margaret, anxious to prevent a collision. "Did you know that Ned Rogers had gone South?"

"I merely heard of it; he owes me twenty-five dollars, the rogue," replied Tom.

"Don't you think you will get it again?" asked Margaret, showing her interest at once.

"Perhaps."

"Well, it will hurt him worse than it will you," said Margaret. "For it only hurts your pocket, and it hurts his reputation."

"Humph! My pocket is worth more to me than his reputation," said Tom, lighting his cigar.

Margaret did not purpose to enter into an argument with her brother; she had only sought to avert the quarrel between him and Clara and had succeeded, so without replying to her brother's last remarks, she hurried off to Mary's room. She found the invalid sitting up and kindly inquired after her health.

"I am ever so much better," said Mary. "I never had my head ache worse, and it never got well so soon before. And I was just thinking, Margaret, that a little nursing does one good sometimes."

"If it has helped you as much as it has me, we will know better how to do another time," said Margaret, picking up the things about the room in an embarrassed way; for such confidence and confessions were entirely new between the sisters. That evening as Mr. and Mrs. Cross sat alone in the sitting room, Mr. Cross inquired after Mary's health.

"She came downstairs after dinner; I guess she is not any worse than usual," said Mrs. Cross.

"It was kind of Margaret to nurse her and wait on her," said Mr. Cross, nervously, for he knew he was treading on dangerous ground.

Mrs. Cross believed little in noticing ailments; it was unwholesome, she said. Children so soon knew how to counterfeit illness. Much to his surprise, she answered, "Yes, Margaret made quite a hero of herself, for all the rest of us are talking about it. I always thought Margaret was more affectionate than any of the rest. More like your sister Alice. There's a difference in people," continued Mrs. Cross. "Some are always a-loving and a-kissing and hanging around somebody, others think as much, but do not care to demonstrate it. Don't you think there's a great difference, Mr. Cross?"

"I'll tell you what I think, Mother. I think there is a difference, but I think folks make it themselves. I believe that God puts warm feelings into every heart, but influences change or develop them. But I think we all stifle these warm impulses too much and allow ourselves to think all demonstrations of tenderness weakly and 'soft' and so crush them out of our hearts, and we freeze up, as it were, until it would take an angel from heaven to thaw us out."

Mr. Cross had grown eloquent in his theme. Mrs. Cross only gave a little sigh, and said, "Well, I don't know, I'm no hand to make a fuss, but I believe I love my children as much as any mother can love her children, but I sometimes think *they* do not think so." Poor mother! She had sown and now was reaping.

"I wish Tom would stay at home evenings," said Margaret, one evening as the sisters were seated at their work, around the center table. "I wonder why boys always want to run off somewhere evenings."

"Because they like rough company, I guess," replied Mary.

"I think they are apt to go where they think they are most appreciated," said Margaret. "We are always scolding at him when he is in the house."

"Well, is it any wonder," said Clara, "when he tangles our worsteds, ridicules our dress, and makes himself a nuisance generally. For my part I am always glad to see him take himself off."

After a long pause, Margaret said, "Mother, may I have that old stove that is out in the shed?"

"What in the world would you do with that?" asked Mrs. Cross, looking in astonishment at her daughter.

"Put it in Tom's room. Perhaps if we fix up his room with a stove and things to make it comfortable he would stay in it more."

"Well, you may try if you wish, but I'm afraid you'll have trouble for your pains."

The next day Margaret went to work. She was not discouraged by the sneers of Clara, nor by the frown of her mother, who said she could see no use of tearing up the house at that time. She tore down the ragged old paper curtains which adorned the windows and substituted neat muslin ones in their place, mended the carpet neatly, put up the old stove, and polished it until it shone again. She cleared the table of its rubbish, of cigar stumps, paper collars, newspapers and shoe brushes; brought a box and gathered up the boots, old and new, and put them into it; found a hanging place for the old clothes which lay scattered on chairs and trunks; and for a last finishing stroke brought up an old rocker which had lost an arm and a round, covered it with an old delaine skirt, padded the back, and placed it beside the stove in which she had arranged a fire. She then took a view of her work. "I think Tom will like this," she said to herself. "At any rate I hope he will."

"Come upstairs, Tom," said she, after dinner, "I have something to show you."

"Bring it down; I'm in a hurry," answered the ungracious Tom.

Margaret laughed. "I can't bring it down. You will have to go where it is," she said, taking his arm and leading the way to his own room.

The fire was burning and shedding a soft light over the narrow passage which led to the room. Tom looked amazed, as Margaret, stopping before the door, said, with mock gravity, "Allow me to introduce your proprietor, Thomas Cross, Esq. We hope you will be mutually pleased with each other."

"This is nice; whose work is this?" inquired the bewildered Thomas, looking around as in a dream.

"Are you pleased with it?"

"Rather."

"Enough to spend your evenings in it?"

"Well, yes, if you'll agree to have a fire for me," said Tom, lazily eyeing the neat room.

"I'll do it!" exclaimed Margaret, clapping her hands gleefully. "And keep you company too, if you will allow me."

It was a mutual agreement, and it proved a happy one to both brother and sister. Together they read their favorite books and discussed their merits. They gave and received confidence and learned all those sweet influences which spring from an intercourse of warm, loving hearts. Nor were these seasons confined to Tom's room. He often sought the family circle, and by his good nature broke away the barriers of reserve and selfishness which had closed around them all. So out of Margaret's resolve and its performance sprang a growth of tenderness that grew and blossomed until every heart in that family was firmly united in the bonds of sympathy and love.

The Talents

Have you read of the servant who hid in the earth
The talent his master had given?
When by diligent use to redouble its worth
He ought to have faithfully striven?

My friend, you have talents—God gave them to you
And will surely require them again;
Take care not to waste them, if ever so few,
Let them not have been given in vain.

You have *Speech;* then remember to watch your words well,
And let them be gentle and kind.
It may seem a small matter, but one can tell
The comfort a word leaves behind.

You have *Time;* every minute and hour of the day,
Is lent by your Father in Heaven,
Make haste to improve ere it passes away,
The talent so graciously given.

You have *Influence,* too, though it seems very small;

Yet in greater of less degree,
You affect the improvement and comfort of all
With whom you may happen to be.

You have talents of *Gold* which by Heaven were lent
Every want of the poor to relieve.
Oh, use them as blessings so graciously sent,
'Tis more blessed to give, than receive.

And the man who is earnest endeavors to live
as an heir of eternity ought,
By his silent *Example* a lesson may give,
Which by words he would never have taught.

Then consider the talents entrusted you,
And may they be duly improved,
Let your service be hearty and free, as is due
From children so greatly beloved.

Taking a Situation

"Well, girls," said my Uncle Barnabas, "and now what do you propose to do about it?"

We sat around the fire in a disconsolate semicircle; Uncle Barnabas Berkelin sat with us erect, stiff, and rather grim. Uncle Barnabas was rich, and we were poor. He was wise in the ways of the world, and we were inexperienced. Uncle Barnabas was prosperous in all he did; while if there was a bad bargain to be made, we were pretty sure to be the ones to make it. Consequently, we looked up to him and reverenced his opinions.

"What do we propose to do about it?" Eleanor slowly repeated. "Yes, that's exactly it," said my mother, nervously; "because, Brother Barnabas, we don't pretend to be business women, and it's certain that we cannot live comfortably on our present income. Something has surely got to be done."

And then my mother leaned back in her chair with a troubled face.

"Yes," said Uncle, "Something has got to be done! But who's to do it?"

And another dread silence succeeded.

"I suppose you girls are educated?' said Uncle Barnabas. "I know I found enough old school bills when I was looking over my brother's papers."

"Of course," said my mother, with evident pride, "their education has been most expensive. Music, drawing, use of globes—"

"Yes, yes, of course," interrupted Uncle Barnabas; "but is it practical? Can they teach?"

Eleanor looked dubious. I was quite sure I could not. Madame Lenoir, among all her list of accomplishments, had not included the art of practical tuition.

"Hump!" grunted Uncle Barnabas. "A queer thing this modern education. Well if you can't teach you can surely do something! What do you say, Eleanor, to a situation?"

"A situation?"

"I spoke plain enough, didn't I?" said Uncle Barnabas, dryly. "Yes, a situation!"

"What sort of situation, Uncle Barnabas?"

"Well, I can hardly say. I guess part servant, part companion to an elderly lady!" explained the old gentleman.

"Oh, Uncle Barnabas, I couldn't do that."

"Not do it? And why not?"

"It's too much—too much," whispered Eleanor, losing her regal dignity in the pressure of the emergency, "like going out to service."

"And that is precisely what it is!" retorted Uncle Barnabas, nodding his head. "Service! Why, we're all out at service, in one way or another, in this world!"

"Oh, yes I know," faltered poor Eleanor, who, between her distaste for the proposed plan and her anxiety not to offend Uncle Barnabas, didn't quite know what to say. "But I—I've always been educated to be a lady."

"So you won't take the position, eh?" said Uncle Barnabas, staring up at a wishy-washy little water-color drawing of Cupid and Psyche—an "exhibition piece" of poor Eleanor's which hung above the chimney piece.

"I couldn't, indeed, sir."

"Wages are twenty-five dollars a month," mechanically repeated Uncle Barnabas, as if he were saying off a lesson. "Drive out in the carriage every day with the missus, cat and canary to take care of, modern house, and all improvements. Sunday afternoons to yourself, and two weeks, spring and fall, to visit your mother."

"No, Uncle Barnabas, no," said Eleanor, with a little shudder. "I am a true Berkelin, and I cannot stoop to menial duties."

Uncle Barnabas gave such a prolonged sniff as to suggest the idea of a very bad cold in his head.

"Sorry," said he. "Heaven helps those who try to help themselves, and you can't expect me to be more liberal-minded than heaven. Sister Rachel," to my mother, "what do you say?"

My mother drew her pretty little figure up a trifle more erect than usual.

"I think my daughter Eleanor is quite right," said she. "The Berkelins have always been ladies."

I had sat quite silent, still with my chin in my hands, during all this family discussion; but now I rose up and came creeping to Uncle Barnabas's side.

"Well, little Susy," said the old gentleman, laying his hand kindly on my wrist, "what is it?"

"If you please, uncle, I would like to take the situation," said I with a throbbing heart.

"Brave!" cried Uncle Barnabas.

"My dear children!" exclaimed my mother.

"Susannah!" uttered Eleanor, in accents by no means laudatory.

"Yes," said I, "twenty-five dollars a month is a great deal of money, and I was never afraid of work. I think I will go to the old lady, Uncle Barnabas. I'm sure I could send home at least twenty dollars a month to mother and Eleanor, and then the two weeks, spring and fall, would be so nice! Please, Uncle Barnabas, I'll go back with you when you go. What is the old lady's name?"

"Her name?" said Uncle Barnabas, "Didn't I tell you? It's Prudence—Mrs. Prudence."

"What a nice name! I know I shall like her," said I.

"Well, I think you will," said Uncle Barnabas, looking kindly at me. "And I think she will like you. Is it a bargain for the nine o'clock train tomorrow morning?"

"Yes," I answered stoutly, taking care not to look in the direction of my mother and Eleanor.

"You're the most sensible of the lot," said Uncle Barnabas, approvingly.

But after he had gone to bed in the best chamber, where the ruffled pillowcases and the chintz-cushioned easy chair were, the full strength of the family tongue broke on my devoted head.

"I can't help it," quoth I, holding valiantly to my color. "We can't starve. Some of us must do something. And you can live very nicely, indeed, mother, darling, on twenty dollars a month."

"That is true," sighed my mother from behind her black-bordered pocket-handkerchief. "But I never thought to see a daughter of mine going out to—service!"

"And Uncle Barnabas isn't going to do anything for us after all," cried out Eleanor, indignantly. "Stingy old fellow; I should think he might at least adopt one of us! He's as rich as Croesus and never a chick nor a child."

"He may do as he likes about that," I answered, independently. "I prefer to earn my own money."

So the next morning I set out for the unknown bourne of New York life.

"Uncle Barnabas, how shall I find where Mrs. Prudence lives?" said I as the train reached the city.

"Oh, I'll go with you," said he.

"Are you well acquainted with her?" I ventured to ask.

"Oh, very well, indeed!" replied Uncle Barnabas, nodding his head approvingly.

We took a carriage at the depot and drove through so many streets that my head spun round and round, before we stopped at a pretty brownstone mansion—it looked like a palace to my unaccustomed eyes—and Uncle Barnabas helped me out.

"Here is where Mrs. Prudence lives," said he with a chuckle.

A neat little maid opened the door, and I was conducted into an elegant apartment, all gilding, exotics and blue satin damask, when a plump old lady, dressed in black silk, came smilingly forward, like a sixty-year-old sunbeam.

"So you've come back, Barnabas, have you," said she, "and brought one of the dear girls with you. Come and kiss me, my dear."

"Yes, Susy, kiss your aunt," said Uncle Barnabas, flinging his hat one way and his gloves another, as he sat complacently down on the sofa.

"My aunt?" I echoed.

"Why, of course," said the plump old lady. "Don't you know? I'm your Aunt Prudence."

"But I thought," gasped I, in bewilderment, "that I was coming to a situation!"

"Well, so you are," retorted Uncle Barnabas. "The situation of adopted daughter in my family. Twenty-five dollars a month pocket money; the care of Aunt Prudence's cat and canary, and to make yourself generally useful."

"Oh! Uncle," cried I, "Eleanor would have been so glad to have come if she had known it."

"Fiddlestrings and little fishes!" illogically responded my uncle. "I've no patience with a girl that's too fine to work. Eleanor had the situation offered to her and chose to decline. You decided to come, and here you stay!"

And this was the way I drifted into my luxurious home. Eleanor in the country cottage envies me bitterly, for she has all the tastes which wealth and a metropolitan home can gratify. But Uncle Barnabas will not hear to my exchange with her. But he lets me send them liberal presents every month, and so I am happy.

Where the Gold Is

Tom Jones was a little fellow and not so quick to learn as some boys, but nobody in the class could beat him in his lessons. He rarely missed in geography, never in spelling, and his arithmetic was always correctly done; as for his reading, no boy improved like him. The boys were fairly angry sometimes; he outdid them so. "Why, Tom, where do you learn your lessons? You don't study in school more than the other boys."

"I rise early in the morning and study two hours before breakfast," answered Tom.

Ah, that is it! "The morning hour has gold in its mouth."

There is a little garden near us, which is the prettiest and most plentiful little spot in all the neighborhood. The earliest radishes, peas, strawberries, and tomatoes grow there. It supplies the family with vegetables, besides some for the market. If anybody wants flowers, that garden is sure for the sweetest roses, pinks and "all sorts" without number. The soil, we used to think, was poor and rocky, besides being exposed to the north wind; and the owner is a busy businessman all day, yet he never hires.

"How do you make so much out of your little garden?"

"I give my mornings to it," answered the owner, "and I don't know which is the most benefited by my work, my garden or myself."

Ah, "the morning hour has gold in its mouth."

William Down was one of our young converts. He united with the church, and appeared well, but I pitied the poor fellow when I thought of his going back to the shipyard to work among a gang of loose associates. "Will he maintain his stand?" I thought. It is so easy to slip back in religion—easier to go back two steps than to advance one. Ah, well, we said, we must trust William to his conscience and his Saviour. Two years passed, and instead of William's losing ground, his piety grew brighter and stronger. Others fell away, but not he, and no boy perhaps was placed in more unfavorable circumstances. Talking with William one evening, I discovered one secret of his steadfastness. "I never, sir, on any account let a single morning pass without secret prayer and the reading of God's word. If I have a good deal to do, I rise an hour earlier. I think over my weak points and try to get God's grace to fortify me just there." Mark this. Prayer is the armor for the battle of life. If you give up your morning petitions you will suffer for it; temptation is before you, and you are not fit to meet it. There is a guilty feeling in the soul, and you keep at a distance from Christ. Be sure the hour of prayer broken in upon by sleepiness can never be made up. Make it a principle, young Christian, to begin the day by watching unto prayer.

"The morning hour has gold in its mouth"; aye, and something better than gold—heavenly gain.

Morning

But who the melodies of morn can tell?
The wild brook babbling down the mountain
side,
The lowing herd—the sheepfold's simple bell;
The pipe of early shepherd dim descried
In the lone valley; echoing far and wide
The clamorous horn along the cliffs above;
The hollow murmur of the ocean tide;
The hum of bees, and the linnet's lay of love,
And the full choir that wakes the universal
grove.

"I Will Do It"

John Corson was a tall, stout boy for his years. He was full of life and spirit as a boy could be, running over with frolic and good feeling and restless energy. Any out-of-door business was his delight. He could skate, fish, row, hoe garden, and drive horses as well, for his age, as the best. He was manly and truthful, too—a noble fellow in his boyish style—that his mother loved, and his father was very proud of. Everybody liked him; I don't know indeed why it should not be so, for he was my ideal of a boy. Only he was not quite perfect, just as nobody in this world is. He had a quick, passionate temper; but that is no fault if it is not allowed to get the mastery of a man. John's temper did sometimes rule him; he had not learned to say "Down!" to the tyrant.

John liked to read. *Robinson Crusoe*, all sorts of war histories, tales of adventure and heroism, and wild, exciting stories were devoured as greedily as a lunch at recess. Oh, how his boy imagination reveled in all dangerous exploits and longed for the dash and the daring of a soldier or a savage!

He went to school, as most boys do, but that was the place he never appeared to the best advantage. He was a favorite in the school yard and was admired for many fine qualities by his teachers, but he did not like to apply himself to a book. His outdoor nature rebelled against the confinement of the schoolroom and the discipline of close, earnest thinking. He was not much of a scholar; I should say, perhaps, such was his reputation, since many boys younger and weaker and less talented than he stood above him in every class study. But really John had all the capacities of a true student, and if he were only diligent, he could have been as far ahead of the majority of the school in mathematics and classics as he was in archery and horsemanship.

Well was it for the boys that his preceptor was a judicious man. He opened no contest with his pupil, but he took with a true eye the measures of his capacity and resolved to inspire him with an ambition he had never felt. For a day or two he waited, watching closely the boy's habits and moods, not as one determined himself to subdue but whose purpose it is to lead the offender, through his own sense of honor and right, to self mastery.

There he sat holding his grammar, feeling as a bird fresh from the wood does the first day in a cage, and putting himself into ill-humor because he could not go off on some rollicking expedition with horse or dog.

He was dreaming of Crusoe life and wishing there were no such things as schoolmasters and Latin verbs.

The bell struck, and John's class was called for recitation. John's lesson was the least understood and the worst recited of the whole. Such a failure was common to John's case. He had been reproved, assisted, and encouraged, but his impatience of discipline left him always far below the standard of his fellows.

The master looked stern the boy—bright, noble and beautiful—stood before him, with his one great failing uppermost over all his young manliness. Mr. L. felt that the hour was a crisis in that young life. He could no longer allow in him the self-indulgence which should leave him weak and superficial in mental requirement; he must teach him to control his restless spirit and to train his mind to think closely, and reason exactly, act within itself in a way to become efficient in all worthy uses.

"John Corson," said Mr. L., "do you want to be a man?"

John smiled and answered promptly, "Yes, sir."

"A whole, true, finished man, John, that can always do whatever he finds to do, being a power in himself—that can fight the bad with the good and be always a victor?"

"Why, yes, sir," said John.

"I thought so; will you please tell me now what makes just such a man?"

John had a pretty good idea of a man; he looked as though he had some pretty strong independent thoughts about it, but he did not know just how to express his thoughts.

"Speak right out, John," said the master; "tell us what you think."

"Why, sir," said John, "a *man* is noble, he don't do anything mean, and he is *somebody*."

"Not a bad definition, my lad; a *man*, you suppose, does his duty, comes right up to the mark, whether it is pleasant to him or not, and makes as much of himself as he can?"

"Yes, sir."

"John, who do you suppose does the most for one toward making a man of him—a man, as you say, that is *somebody*?"

"I don't know, sir, unless it is his father."

"A good father helps a great deal—a good teacher also; good companions and good books also help very much; but the work is done chiefly by the man himself. It is self work, such as none other can do for him—more than everything else together. God gives one a being full of capacities to be developed and strengthened and enlarged—all good and right, you know—but they must be very carefully guarded and educated so as to do the best work and the most of it and in the best manner. Some have more in themselves upon which to build a fine manhood than others; but it is for everyone to say for himself how much of a man he shall be—whether little or noble—nobody or somebody. Did you ever think of this, John?"

"Not very much, I guess."

"So I supposed. You see how it is—one must be determined to correct the bad traits of character if he would become a good man. His too strong points, like a hasty, disagreeable temper, he must subdue and keep down because it is not noble to be overcome of a harsh and hateful passion; the weak places he must teach and train and strengthen as much as he can, or there will be great defects to shame and hinder him. The slack places he must take special care of. If there is anything in his duties of learning or training he does not like to do, he must gird his will and his resolution right up to see that he does not lose his chance of being a man just then.

"You have some nice accomplishments, John, and I am glad for it. They will help you to be a man, and you can be as brave and noble in many things as any boy I know, and that makes me proud and happy. But, oh, the slack spot, John! Do you know where it is?"

"It is about the lesson, I suppose," said John.

"Yes. Here you are, a bright, strong boy, ready to walk right up to a true, finished manhood if you will;

but you come here day after day and sit restlessly and idly, with your hands full of true and important and beautiful work, which you leave half done because you are too slack to do it. You don't want to grow strong and large in intellect, to learn the best ideas of the noblest minds, to reason and compare and calculate because it costs an effort you are not fond of now. And I never feel that my pupil, with all his talent for being somebody, is sure to become a noble man, full grown in mind and soul, because he does not take his work with a right manly courage and say, *I will do it!*

"You see, the battle is all to yourself, John, and nobody can fight it out but you—the battle between duty and discipline on one side and ill-tempered slackness on the other. How shall it be? Will you conquer the lessons and so grow efficient in mind and manly in will? Or shall the lessons conquer you while your intellect lies weak and untrained, and your manhood becomes only a dwarf to the strong, brave character it can as well grow to as not? In this great life battle, will you be a common soldier or an officer fit to command yourself and to lead other men?"

John could not bear to think of being less of a man; he saw and was ashamed of his weakness. But he did not say much that day, and Mr. L. left him to his own meditations.

The next day John came to school and sat down to his duties.

"Well, my lad," said the master, very kindly, "have you decided who shall conquer?"

"*I will do it!*" answered John, promptly and nobly; "please, sir, see if I don't!"

"That is the point to be gained, John; hold to it, and I expect you to be a man."

Oh, it was hard work, sometimes—uphill work for a while, but John Corson persevered and conquered. All the boy's better nature was enlisted; the new motive, the manly aim, accomplished the master's ideas. Mr. L. became proud of his pupil.

I wish you could see John now that ten years are added to his age—ten years of close study and earnest thinking and doing. He has been looking carefully to the weak places and the slack places, for which he has reaped an honorable and glorious award. He *is somebody*, and whoever looks upon his intelligent face and manly figure acknowledges it.

John Corson will never forget that schoolmaster; he loves him with a noble friendship and thanks God that there was one to inspire at the right moment with a right ambition. I think, also, that Mr. L. was never more grateful that God had given him some true work to do than when a few years ago John called on his old teacher to express his gratitude for the few kind words that startled him out of his indolence and set before him a true and noble endeavor.

"Conquer or be conquered, as you spoke the word that afternoon," said he, "has stood by me ever since."

"Rather say," replied Mr. L., "that the '*I will do it!*' you uttered the next morning has carried you through."

Boys, take up the "*I will do it,*" fill out the pattern of your best, noblest being, and see if that is far different from, or much less than, genius!

The Little Weaver

At a great sacrifice, a little maiden was once rescued from cruel bondage by a noble and powerful king. Many others had been ransomed in like manner, and the monarch extended to them all an invitation to unite in a grand jubilee to celebrate their liberation.

These captives wrought at the loom, and the king bade each weave a beautiful robe to wear to the great feast. If the work was faithfully performed, he promised to receive them into his own palace as members of the royal family.

Filled with love and gratitude to her deliverer, the little maiden eagerly began her task. Day after day, the shuttle flew swiftly to and fro, weaving, in a pure white groundwork, beautiful figures of bright blue and shining gold.

As time passed on, she grew weary; the syren's song fell sweetly on her ear, and soon she left her toil to join the giddy throng of worshipping at pleasure's shrine. But she found their fair exterior covering oft an aching heart; sharp, cruel thorns were hidden 'neath the roses wreathed around her brow, and the silver-hued illusions vanished from her grasp. Then she remembered him who had redeemed her at so great a price and turned back to her task again. Alas? An enemy had been at work. There were dark stains on the white groundwork, and the golden threads were tarnished. With bitter tears of penitence she confessed her wanderings and hastened to the fountain where the soiled fabric might be made pure once more. No longer could the gayety around attract her notice, for beyond the distant hills her fancy saw the sunlight gleaming on the palace walls, and with new courage she plied the shuttle.

Sometimes her cunning foe would steal the golden thread and substitute a false tinsel, but it was detected by the test—the precious guidebook which the king had given—and she carefully removed it, for a single thread would mar the garment and bar her forever from her promised home.

In every time of need the king provided help, and still she persevered. Others who had dropped their shuttles, now resumed them, once more sought the golden thread, and washed their defiled garments in the all-cleansing fountain. A few of the gay revelers, attracted by her glad songs and cheering words of the bright land afar, turned from their folly and joined her in the service of the master.

At last the work was done. The king, with all his retinue, came to receive his faithful servants. With joy, and yet in fear, the maiden went to meet him. Deeply she felt her own unworthiness and timidly advancing fell at his feet as he received the fabric she had wrought. He gazed with loving tenderness on the bowed form before him and gently bade her rise again, "Thou has done well the work which I commanded, and behold, I have received thee"; then he passed his hand over the garment, and the tears that had fallen here and there became pure, shining pearls. Throwing over it a transparent, silvery covering of dazzling brightness, he cast the robe around her, placed in her hand a harp, and on her brow a glittering crown, where, for everyone whom she had led to serve the king, a star shone now.

Oh! Pen may not describe, or artist picture, the beauty of that land which was to be the home of the redeemed; and as they reached its shining portals, the king himself threw back the palace gates and bade them enter in, amid the glories there, to dwell forevermore.

Dear reader, this is no fancy sketch. We are all working at the loom. Let us weave, for our robe of character, the spotless white of purity, the clear, bright blue of truth, and the golden thread of love to God and man. Let us beware of the tinsel of selfishness, for it can never enter the Holy City. Let us set a guard over ourselves lest in a thoughtless hour we weave threads soiled and spotted with envy, deceit and kindred evils; for only a character formed by a life of faithful obedience to God and cleansed by the atoning blood of

Christ can receive that glorious covering—His righteousness.

The Loom of Life

All day, all night, I can hear the jar,
Of the loom of life, and near and far
It thrills with its deep and muffled sound,
As the tireless wheels go always around.
Busily, ceaselessly goes the loom,
The wheels are turning early and late,
And the woof is wound in the warp of fate.

Click, clack! There's a thread of love wove in!
Click, clack! And another of wrong and sin;
What a checkered thing will this life be,
When we see it unrolled in eternity!

Time, with a face like a mystery,
And hands as busy as hands can be,
Sits at the loom with its warp outspread,
To catch in its meshes each glancing thread.
When shall this wonderful web be done?
In a thousand years? Perhaps in one;
Or tomorrow. Who knoweth! Not you nor I,
But the wheels turn on, and the shuttles fly.

Ah, sad-eyed weaver, the years are slow,
But each one is nearer the end, I know.
And some day the last thread shall be woven in,
God granted it be love instead of sin.
Are we spinners of woof for this life-web—
say?
Do we furnish the weaver a thread each day?
It were better then, oh my friend, to spin
A beautiful thread, than a thread of sin.

The Garden of Peace

In an ancient city of the East, two youths were passing a beautiful garden. It was closed by a lofty trellis, which prevented their entering, but, through the openings they could perceive that it was a most enchanting spot. It was embellished by every object of nature and art that could give the beauty to the landscape. There were groves of lofty trees, with winding avenues between them; there were green lawns, the grass of which seemed like velvet; there were groups of shrubs, many of them in bloom, and scattering delicious fragrance upon the atmosphere.

Between these pleasing objects, there were fountains sending their silvery showers into the air, and a stream of water, clear as crystal, wound with gentle murmurs through the place. The charms of this lovely scene were greatly heightened by the delicious music of birds, the hum of bees, and the echoes of many youthful and happy voices.

The two young men gazed upon the scene with intense interest; but, as they could only see a portion of it through the trellis, they looked about for some gate by which they might enter the garden. At a little distance they perceived a gateway, and they went to the spot, supposing they should find an entrance there.

There was, indeed, a gate; but it was locked, and they found it impossible to gain admittance.

While they were considering what course they should adopt, they perceived an inscription over the gate, which ran as follows:

"Ne'er till tomorrow's light delay
What may as well be done today;
Ne'er do the thing you'd wish undone,
Viewed by tomorrow's rising sun.
Observe these rules a single year,
And you may safely enter here."

The two youths were very much struck by these lines, and, before they parted, both agreed to make the experiment by trying to live according to the inscription.

I need not tell the details of their progress in the trial; both found the task much more difficult than they at first imagined. To their surprise, they found that an observance of the rule they had adopted required an almost total change of the modes of life. And this taught them what they had not felt before, that a very large part of their lives—a very large share of their thoughts, feelings, and actions—were wrong, though they were considered virtuous young men by the society in which they lived.

After a few weeks, the younger of the two, finding that the scheme put too many restraints upon his tastes, abandoned the trial. The other persevered, and, at the end of the year, he presented himself at the garden.

To his great joy he was freely admitted; and if the place pleased him when seen dimly through the trellis, it appeared far more lovely now that he could actually tread its pathways, breathe its balmy air, and mingle intimately with the scenes around.

This garden fitly represents the happy home promised to those who conquer selfishness, those who conquer their passions, and do their duty. The tall gateway is the barrier interposed by human vices and human passions, which separates mankind from the peace, of which we are all capable. Whoever can conquer himself and has resolved firmly that he will do it, has found the key to that gate, and he may freely enter here. If he cannot do that, he must continue to be an outcast from the Garden of Peace.

She Is Unkind to Her Mother

"My son," said an aged father to his promising boy, as he discovered his increasing interest in the daughter of his neighbor, "Weigh well in this matter. I am an old man, and have not been an idle observer of the human family during my long life. One misstep taken now may ruin your prospects of happiness for this life or so mar it as to render life almost undesirable. Many young men have made shipwreck of their peace by unadvisedly and unjudiciously contracting an alliance of matrimony with woman of bad dispositions."

"Why, Father," interrupted Charles, "you are putting me quite aback by speculating in so serious a manner, upon what I thought so agreeable a subject, as to excite my apprehensions and awaken my fears. I have not designedly kept anything secret from you; my visits to neighbor B.'s have all been known and never disapproved of to my knowledge."

"No, my son," continued the father, "you have not acted covertly or unfilially in this matter. This gives me increasing confidence in you. I have noticed, and with pain too, your oft-repeated visits to Mr. B.'s and have as often desired to caution you, but have been waiting a suitable opportunity. The best evidence, I think, a father can give to his son of his love and his confidence in him, is the plainness and candor with which he makes known to him his mind upon all subjects. To be honest, then, you must allow me to say that you are mistaken in Miss B.'s worthiness of your affections. She is not the young lady your imagination has painted. I am sure that you would not, upon this or any other subject, act in direct opposition to sentiments you have habitually expressed."

"Why, Father," exclaimed Charles, "you seem more and more serious."

"Have I not, my son, again and again heard you say that you would not marry any young lady who is unkind to her mother or who was disrespectful to her?"

"Yes, Father," hastily answered Charles, "those are my sentiments and always will be, but I was not aware that there could be any application of them in the present case. Miss B. has always appeared exceedingly mild and pleasant when in my company and always treated her mother, for aught I knew, with propriety."

"Ah, my son, your affection has thrown a mantle over her conduct. She has wounded us all. Old people look at these things dispassionately. Your mother and myself have often spoken, when alone, of Miss B.'s unkind treatment of her mother. We have seen her give her mother such glances and heard her make such tart answers, when she was not suited, as to cause our hearts to ache. Miss B. has too much sense, and values our esteem too much, to come right out before us and tell her mother to 'hold her tongue'; or that 'she does not know what she is talking about'; and such like. But her natural good sense had not power enough over her bad natural disposition to suppress those glances, those intonations of voice, and those short answers which her too sensitive mother understood."

"But, Father, Mary has much to contend with. Her mother, you know, is not the most intelligent woman in the world, and sometimes things occur very mortifying to Mary. She, having been sent abroad and becoming educated in a very superior manner, finds it sometimes a very difficult task to put up with her mother's lack of modern improvement."

"That argument, Charles," rejoined the father, "if of any weight, goes directly against Miss B. because she should be more tender and forbearing, kind and respectful to her mother, so as to hide, if possible, her imperfections. It is a hard case, my son, that a daughter, because she has had superior advantages and become more accomplished than her mother, should set herself above her. In those very advantages and accomplishments should be laid the basis of heartfelt gratitude, respect and affection. What! Treat her own mother with unkindness and neglect in company, especially before those in whose eyes she should endeavor to exalt her? Who was it, Charles, that watched over Mary from her earliest infancy, bore with fretfulness and troublesomeness of her early childhood? Who was it that guarded her health, watched over her by day and by night, and often again, with whether she breathed in health? Who was it that wept when Mary's skin was hot, her breath feverish, and her pulse quick and hard? Who was it that bathed her temples, prepared for her every little delicacy, and hung over her as an angel ministering to her wants? Whose eyes were those that beamed with delight as Mary gradually arose from her sick bed and became restored to health? And last, though not least, who was it that bowed with Mary at the throne of grace, when her little lips could scarcely articulate and taught her to lisp the name of Jesus? Was it not her own mother? The same mother she can now treat with neglect and unkindness. Beware, my son! We know Miss B. is unquestionably a young lady of fine talents, and superior education. She has a fine, commanding person. She is of a highly respectable genteel family. All these things are desirable. But she lacks one thing—an amiable disposition. She is unkind to her mother, and my experience has always taught me that an unkind daughter habitually makes an unkind wife."